WEDDING BELLS & PSYCHIC SPELLS

CONFESSIONS OF A CLOSET MEDIUM
BOOK 8

NYX HALLIWELL

Beach Path Publishing LLC

ONE

"Why is Kit lying on our lawn?" I ask Logan.

We pull into a space in front of my business, The Wedding Chapel, and he puts his Porsche into park. We stare at our newest friend, a private detective with strong psychic abilities, who lies spread-eagle on the grassy yard. Orange and yellow maple leaves float in the breeze, lazily spiraling over her. One wings itself in our direction and catches in my hair, thanks to the fact the convertible's top is down. It's a warm fall day in late October, too warm for Halloween but perfect for our wedding ceremony taking place in two days.

He squints his blue eyes behind his aviator sunglasses, shutting off the engine. "What's on her head?"

Not a leaf, that's for sure. My brain is so overwhelmed with details about our official nuptials and the huge reception, I struggle to place what kind of crystal is sparkling in the center of her forehead. "An amethyst?"

Kit doesn't move, yet calls, "I can hear you, you know."

We exit the car, Logan retrieving the shopping and

garment bags from the tiny backseat. The gate is open and I eye Kit as I approach, frowning at her rumpled clothes and the dark circles under her closed eyes. Having been on my own sleep roller coaster for the past month in preparation for the grandest event to take place in Thornhollow since, well, *ever*, I consider joining her and calling it a day. "We have a spare room if you want to take a nap."

Her eyes stay clamped shut. "Just leave me be."

A group of smartly dressed women sip drinks on the porch across the street at Tea Leaves, my friend, Sage's, shop. I'm certain from the way they've fallen silent that this incident will be all over town by dinner. Logan passes me, hauling my new trousseau to the porch. He lifts a brow as he goes past and I shrug. Kit's been upset for weeks due to trouble with one of my least favorite things—ghosts.

Even as I refuse to glance at an unknown one peeking at me from the corner of the house, I feel a ripple of frigid, otherworldly air tease my face and slide down my spine. The elderly gentleman wears a hat and suit that went out of style a hundred years ago. He shouldn't be able to cross the warded perimeter I've established with salt lines and charmed crystals but I'll deal with him later. I crouch next to Kit and lower my voice. "Is it still happening?"

"That's why I'm here," she grumbles. "This is the nexus. If I could just clear it, the spooks would stop haunting me."

I hesitate. "The nexus of what?"

"The town's grid. In any place where people gather there is a collection of energy that, over time, forms a matrix of memories. This plot of ground is at the center of it." She squeezes her eyes tighter. "I'm trying to clear it so it stops creating a blockage with the spirits. There are layers and layers of ghosts and other *things*. Time loops and threads that go nowhere, like a broken spider's web. Probably caused by magic workers who didn't know what they were doing. They left fragments all over the place, and it's causing earthbound spirits to get drawn here."

This is news to me, but it makes sense. My many-times great-grandparents founded Thornhollow, and their original home sits on the property at the bottom of the hill. "Is there anything I can do?"

"Leave me alone for now. I need to untangle more threads."

The sharp-eared pack across the street disguised as Southern belles are all friends with my mother-in-law and will be reporting this to her before I can get inside the house. Although Logan and I are technically married after doing a handfasting ceremony in June, we've agreed to a second, traditional one to make her happy. She insisted on October thirty-first since the grape harvest is complete and she and his father tied the knot on the same day thirty-five years ago.

I consider doing as Kit wants. Then decide I might as well give the wolves something worth reporting. "Would you like company?"

Kit peeks open one eye at me. "What?"

"I may not be psychic, but I *am* your friend." I settle on the ground, adjusting my skirt and kicking off my heels. "If you want to get close to the nexus, I'd suggest taking a walk out back. It's probably under Samuel and Tabitha's homestead. I can take you to it if you want."

She sighs, opening the other eye and staring up at the sky. "If I could only untangle this ball of ghostly energy, I think I'd be less afflicted."

I stand, brushing grass off my pants, and snagging my shoes, offering her a hand. The hovering ghost at the corner of the house slinks into the shadows when I shoot him a glare. "How about some sweet tea, or maybe a cider, before we tackle that?"

Wearily, she accepts my help and rises, palming the crystal. "Got anything stronger?"

"My husband is Logan Cross III. Our house is never dry. Come on."

The front door swings open and my high school intern, Lia, bounds out, her hair dyed a bright orange in honor of the holiday. "Jenn and I are off to the vineyard to start decorating. Are you coming? I hope the ghosts are there. I'm bringing my equipment." She pats the tote slung on her shoulder.

I need to oversee the decorating of the immense barn that will host the reception. It was once a speakeasy, and as my young ghost-obsessed friend has discovered, it is indeed haunted by spirits who lived and died in the area during Prohibition and The Depression. As a medium, I've been able to send a few to the afterlife, but the rest are stubborn, refusing to move on. I had hoped to be rid of all of the earthbound spirits before Saturday, but even on my wedding day, I'm going to be plagued by the dead.

Which is why I understand Kit's exhaustion and distress and decide I need to help her first. "You and Jenn go on. I'll catch up as soon as I can." I wave at the crowd, plastering a smile on my face as I lower my voice. "And keep your ghost-hunting paraphernalia out of sight, or St. Helen will throw a fit."

Lia gives a mock salute. "Aye, aye, Captain Ghost Whisperer. I'll keep my investigation on the down low, but she avoids me, so no worries. I think she's scared of me."

Helen Cross isn't scared of anyone. She isn't even frightened of spirits. The vineyard is Logan's heritage, and his mother runs it with a head for business and a no-nonsense attitude about her place as a leader in our quaint town. While my mother, Dixie, is Thornhollow's mayor, my mother-in-law holds equal sway over the community.

Jenn appears, lugging bags of decorations. She also sports orange hair, hers with black stripes. She has a new piercing in her left brow. "Ready?" she asks.

Lia skips down the steps. "She's not coming."

"I need to show Kit the old homestead first." I guide my friend across the threshold. "I'll meet you two in a bit."

Jenn steers her cargo between the gargoyle banisters as she follows Lia. "Are we seating six or eight at the round tables?"

"We have to do banquet tables because there are so many guests. Logan set up fifteen in the barn, including the bridal party's at the front. We'll seat six on each side of those. We need the rest under the big tent outside, but will have to leave decorating it until the day of."

"Okie dokie. See you in a few."

Inside, I set my purse on my desk, petting my two cats who lounge in the display window, before I point Kit to the kitchen. Rosie is on the phone with a client and Logan has taken my gown and purchases upstairs. I nod at Rosie as I pass and she hands me a stack of messages. Her chihuahua, Fern, peeks at me from her bed near Rosie's feet.

Kit is in our liquor cabinet, surveying the contents when I enter. "I probably shouldn't imbibe. Screws up my gift."

That may be the case but she still adds a generous shot of vodka to the glass of tea I pour for her, along with a squeeze of lemon. She offers the bottle to me, but I wave it away. "I'm sorry this is happening to you. Maybe you need to get out of town."

"And leave you here with this mess?" She makes a dismissive sound in her throat and takes a swig of her drink. "You have enough going on at the moment. I'll figure this out, one way or another."

Thumbing through the slips, I see I missed a call from my mother and another from the Chamber of Commerce Vice President, Baylor Davis, concerning the fall festival parade on Friday. I wonder why my mom didn't call my cell. Maybe she did. I haven't looked at it in hours since I can't locate it.

I try not to appear as stressed as I feel, realizing that I haven't prepared the opening speech for the parade to kick off the festival. As president, it's my responsibility to kick off the festivities. I'll have to recruit Mama to do it for me. She's better at public speaking, anyway.

I snag a brownie from the plastic container on the counter, thankful my next-door neighbor, Rhys, is a great cook and he's always dropping off food. These are double chocolate with a homemade fudge frosting that he should patent. I offer the goodies to Kit and she helps herself to two. My kind of gal.

We eat in comfortable silence, and while my brain is full of all the responsibilities stacked up in front of me, I wonder what is going on in her head. "I'm worried about you."

She takes a big bite and chews slowly as if she wants to choose her response carefully. "I've experienced some weird stuff in my life, but nothing like this."

I've experienced bizarre situations myself when it comes to ghosts, as well as people. "We'll figure it out."

I carry what's left of my snack and drink to the back

door, staring out the window toward my grandparents' house. Usually, the minute I'm in the kitchen, all the cats come running, including my shapeshifter grandmother, who spends most of her time as a tabby cat. Since her husband is a ghost who's promised to cross over after he sees me walk down the church aisle, I imagine the two of them are spending as much time together as possible before the ceremony. Hopefully, when Kit and I get down there, Tabitha is not running around naked, as is her penchant when in her human form. She has absolutely no modesty, and being a Scottish witch of some renown, claims I'm a prude.

Movement along the tree line to my right catches my eye. At first, I assume it's Rhys coming over to check on me. I hope he's bringing more brownies.

Instead of him, I catch sight of a phantom figure disappearing behind the gazebo. I narrow my eyes and stare harder, wondering if it's my grandfather or the ghost I saw hanging around the corner of the house. Samuel is obviously welcome here; other spirits are not. "Stay put," I tell Kit. "Let me check something before we walk down."

Busy eating and drinking, she simply nods.

A chill descends on me and I rub my arms as I traverse the yard. The temperature drops more and a pressure starts in the back of my head. At the bottom of the hill, the old homestead stands, serene and quiet, the trickling stream a soft, white noise, along with the rustling leaves. Clouds have gathered overhead, making the afternoon shadowed. As I halt and survey the area, the landscape goes monochrome, my Aunt Willa's prized rose bushes drained of color, the white gazebo, gray.

"What is going on?" I mutter under my breath. It's as if I've stepped into an old black-and-white film, and my chest gets tight. The back of my neck throbs, sending spikes of icy heat into my skull.

As I try to blink away the filmy haze coating the landscape, I hear a rustle. Faint and breathy, it's like a sigh. My blood runs cold, matching my skin, and suddenly everything comes into clearer contrast. There's still little color around me, but I can see every detail.

The reason for the cold gray landscape lines the perimeter. Hundreds of vacant, dead eyes stare at me. Bodies of the thinnest phantom fog hover and flicker in and out.

As I watch, they cross my warded property lines, closing in.

Ghosts.

And they're coming for me.

TWO

"Ava?"

Logan's voice is a balm, snapping me out of the horrible scene. The normal world flickers back into view.

No ghosts. No gray film. No clouds overhead. The sun is warm on my face as I turn to him, feeling as if I've emerged from a nightmare. It fades just as quickly as one, but I struggle to understand what he's saying to me as he strides toward me.

"Are you okay? You look like you've seen a..." He catches himself before he says the word.

Ghost. It hangs between us like a falling leaf suspended on the breeze.

I glance over my shoulder at the yard, the tree line, the gazebo. They're all gone. "Must be the stress getting to me," I tell him, rubbing my forehead. "I'm fine."

I see the doubt etched on his face. My smile does little to quell it but he holds up two ties. "Which do you prefer with my tweed jacket?"

I point to the forest green with yellow specks. "That one."

He kisses my cheek. "Thanks. Me, too."

The screen door opens and Rosie leans out. "There are two gentlemen here to see you."

"Me?" I ask.

She points at Logan. "You. They don't have an appointment."

Together we head to the porch. Logan hangs the green tie around his neck as we climb the steps. "Did they say who they are?"

"Drew Hurley. Says he went to school with you. The other appears to be his father."

"Drew?" Logan holds the door for me. "I haven't seen him in at least ten years."

I have no idea who he is, but the name Hurley rings a bell. Inside, I find Kit asleep at the table, her folded arms forming a pillow under her head. Soft snores are interrupted by indecipherable murmurs.

Logan is the only lawyer in our town and uses the former den as his office. He goes to the foyer and I stop at Rosie's desk to get a peek at our unexpected visitors.

She leans in and speaks softly. "Your mother says you're not answering your cell. Did you lose it again?"

"I haven't seen it since I was at the vineyard this morning."

"Drew." Logan holds out a hand as he greets the man loitering by the door. Fern dances around Rosie's desk, growling and shaking, as she always does when excited, nervous, or has to pee. Moxley, Logan's basset hound, rouses himself from his afternoon nap and stands near her, licking her face as though to let her know he'll defend her if necessary. "It's been ages! What are you doing here?"

The guy has to be seven feet tall, and indeed looks like a slimmer version of the older man next to him. Drew grabs Logan, bringing him in for a manly hug and slap on the back. "There he is, Dauntless Cross. How are you, man?"

"Good, and you?"

"Can't complain. I'm in town for the festival, and Dad wanted to talk to you about a proposition. Thought we'd come by and see what you were up to."

Logan offers a hand to the older man. "Dean Hurley, nice to see you again. Are you still holding the reins at Creighton U?"

"I am." They shake and he glances my way, then past my shoulder, scanning the large, open rooms. "I thought your office was across the street, and now I see that's a tea shop. The owner said you live and work here now."

Logan waves me forward. "Dr. Hurley, Drew, this is my wife, Ava. She owns the house and runs an event planning business. She's also a wedding gown designer." He motions to the men. "Ava, this is Drew and Howard Hurley. Drew and I played at CU. He was picked up by the Atlanta Hawks."

"Nice to meet you." Now I know why the Dean's name is familiar. He's head of the private college Logan attended for his undergrad studies. Creighton University specializes in law, architecture, and business.

Drew looks me over. "You conquered the heart of the great Dauntless." He takes my hand, bowing over it. "You're a legend."

Logan smacks his shoulder and we all laugh. Drew releases his grip, his grin contagious.

"I assume by that statement," I say, "there is a story I need to hear."

"More than one." He winks and makes a phone receiver with his finger and thumb. "Anytime you're up for it, call me."

Logan steers the men toward the rear of the main floor. "Let's have a seat in my office." I know he doesn't have time for this but like me with Kit, he's making time. He's due to meet his brother, Chuck. They are heading to an indoor climbing place before playing poker at the country club with their usual posse. "I want to hear about this proposition. And then you should come to my bachelor party tonight. Chuck will get a kick out of seeing you."

Drew appears dumbfounded, glancing at me. "I thought you were already married."

I chuckle. "Long story. He'll explain later. You play poker?"

"Not as well as basketball."

"We won't take up much of your time," the dean states. His voice is slow, sugary, southern politeness, but it has a steel edge under it now. As if he doesn't plan to take no for an answer. "I find myself in need of a law professor. A temporary position, mind you, but could lead to something more permanent down the road."

"I am happy to recommend a few potential candidates," Logan says.

"You filled in for Dr. Rhodes last year." Howard gives him a nod as if this clears up any confusion. I can tell by his posture and voice, that he is not one to beat around the bush, nor does he take to people telling him no. "I wish to discuss you returning to do so again."

Logan's face falls with the surprise of the offer. He has big plans in the works for his future, and I can't imagine this could fit into them, but an image of him as a college professor flits through my mind. With his intellect and patience, he would make a great teacher.

On the other hand, Creighton is forty miles away and I would miss having him around. With him being the lone lawyer in town, I wouldn't be the only one.

The phone on Rosie's desk rings. I need to get to my own office and call my mother. Maybe Kit will sleep a bit longer. "Can I get you all something to drink?"

The dean nods. "Water, please."

"Nothing for me," Drew answers.

The two men start to follow Logan when Dr. Hurley freezes as he glances past me. "Kathryn?"

Kit stands in the doorway, looking like someone has punched her in the gut. "Howie? What are you doing here?"

His features harden. "I was about to ask you the same."

Her face is too pale, emphasizing the dark circles under them. I march next to her and put an arm around her waist. "You two know each other?"

Even Drew looks shocked at seeing her.

Dr. Hurley opens his mouth to answer, then shuts it, and turns on his heel, leaving the door open as he exits.

Kit does a similar thing, flying through the kitchen and out the back. The screen slams in her wake.

Drew, Logan, and I simply stare at each other. "What just happened?" he asks.

"She a friend of yours?" Drew peers after his father who has made it to the sidewalk and is climbing into a green Jaguar. "I had no idea."

"Why is that a big deal?" I inquire.

Drew shakes his head, leaving. "Because Kit Lyons broke up my mom and dad's marriage."

THREE

I find Kit by the stream. Tabby weaves around her ankles, her orange tail caressing her legs as my friend stares across the ravine seeing nothing. Her cheeks are damp from tears and when she realizes I'm approaching, she dashes the backs of her hands across them.

Allowing her a moment, I keep quiet and listen to the burble of the water. The fall has been dry and the water is low. A year ago, my aunt died in this spot and my life changed forever. I brought her killers to justice, but I say a silent prayer for her as I watch leaves get carried past us, knocking into rocks and the bank, steep with the water so low.

"The grid is certainly tangled here," Kit says. "It feels dammed up."

I'm more interested in how tangled her relationship is with the two men I just met. "Do you think you can unblock it?"

She makes a weary groan. "I'm not sure. My head is"—she rubs her temples—"all snarled up, too."

"Do you want to talk about it?"

"About the fact my third eye is freaking out with unwanted thoughts and images, or about my past and the mistakes I've made?"

"Either. Both." I watch Tabby as she peers up the hill. I glance in that direction, but luckily, see nothing out of the ordinary. No ghosts or weird shadows. "You know, we've all made mistakes."

"Yeah, well, I'm psychic. You'd think I could see enough of my own future not to screw up so badly and do irreparable damage to someone else's life."

Tough to counter that. "Did you love him?"

A long, sad pause hangs in the cool air between us. "I did. His wife didn't. In fact, she was trying to kill him. That I saw." She taps the center of her forehead. "Here."

My brain puts a few of the pieces together. "You warned him. He didn't know about your ability?"

She gives a bitter laugh and turns to focus on the farmhouse as Tabby strolls toward it. My grandfather hovers in the doorway, staring at us with a questioning expression on his spectral face. "We have more important things to do than stand here and feel sorry for me."

I walk with her to the house, its foundation now shored up, the windows, doors, and roof replaced, thanks to Evander Quigg and his son, Bisby. It's taken all spring and summer to complete those tasks, even with them working around the clock. Restoration of such an old, historic building like this is a challenge. Work is stalled for this week since Evan and Bis are out of town on family business. "You're sure there's nothing I can do to help?"

"Not yet. Maybe later."

"Greetings," Samuel calls. Tabby pads past him inside

and he watches her go with longing in his eyes. "Are you here about the ghosts?"

Kit tilts her head. "What ghosts?"

"You saw them, too?" I point toward the gazebo. "Earlier, over there?"

Samuel eyes me quizzically. "Sorry, no. I was referring to those haunting the speakeasy."

"Oh." Maybe I did imagine the previous horde. "I do need help crossing some of them. They don't want to go. Others are simple stuck loops, no consciousness involved. The ghosts simply continue to repeat the moments surrounding their deaths. Not sure what to do with those. I could use your advice. I'm out of time and I can't enjoy the reception with them hanging around."

Samuel beams. "I'm most happy to assist. Sherlock and I have a plan."

As long as it works, I'm willing to let my grandfather and his ghost friend, who believes he is the fictional character of literary legend, do whatever they like. "At least you two are here for me. Persephone certainly isn't." My guardian angel is AWOL, as per normal.

Kit stares in the direction of the hill. "When did you see these other ghosts?" She faces me. "How many were there?"

"A lot. It must be the stress getting to me. I've been so worried about them wrecking my wedding day, I'm hallucinating."

"Tell me exactly what happened," Kit demands.

By the look on her face, she won't take no for an answer. Begrudgingly, I relate my experience. "Everything was odd, the landscape, the sky, it was all gray and white. The spirits were angry and they were going to attack me. Then Logan came out, and they disappeared. He didn't even realize what was happening." I glance at the cloudy sky. Goosebumps trickle over my skin. "Crazy, right?"

"Oh dear," My grandfather says, distressed.

"Oh, dear," Kit echoes.

I feel queasy at their expressions. "What?"

"Things are out of sorts." My grandmother appears in human form and leans on the doorpost. Her red hair and green eyes are a tribute to her ancestry. At least she's wearing clothes, albeit the jeans and yellow shirt with butterflies were last in *my* closet. "There's a storm a-brewin' as sure as the potions in Cerridwen's cauldron."

"What does that mean?" I probably don't want to know. "Whatever it is, can't it wait until after Saturday?"

Her intense gaze is somber. "Afraid not, granddaughter."

Kit looks ill. "This is all my fault."

"What is?" I demand. "What's happening?"

"You're the magnet and the blockade," Tabitha says. "Sounds like the earthbound are coming for you, and they won't stop until ye be one of them."

FOUR

The chill on my skin sinks into my bones. "Why me?"

"Because of me," Kit replies. "I haven't destroyed the knot in the grid. Everything is being drawn here, to this place, to you."

Tabitha pushes off the frame and gestures for us to come inside. "The veil is thin, and the presence of myself, Samuel, and Ava, all three of us powerful magic workers, is a battery for them."

I point at my chest. "Not a magic worker." Not intentionally, anyway. I'd love to leave the ghost-whispering business behind. "I just see and hear spirits."

Tabitha waves me off. "The property itself is steeped in magic and power. Always has been. It's one of the reasons I chose it for our home."

We start to enter the farmhouse, but Rosie's voice rings out over the lawn. "Ava! Your mom is on line one. You better talk to her. She sounds like she's about to have an aneurysm."

Tabitha sinks into the shadows, out of the sight line of the back porch where Rosie stands, hailing me. "Go," my many-times great-grandmother says. "We'll discuss what can be done to solve the problem."

Mama's timing couldn't be worse. "I'll be back in a minute," I promise.

When Rosie sees me heading her way, she hustles back inside, the screen door flapping closed. As I near the gazebo, the temperature drops and my feet slow, an uncanny breeze whispering about my head. Gooseflesh rises on the back of my neck and I feel that crushing weight at the base of my skull. I chance a peek at the structure and see a silvery spirit hovering inside. A young woman, maybe nineteen, twenty years old. She wears a plain nightgown, soiled with a dark stain. Her hands rest on her pregnant belly. "Help me."

The world turns icy white and steel gray. The press of unseen apparitions closes off my throat and traps the breath inside my chest. *Who are you?*

Her solemn brown eyes bore into mine. *He left me. Why doesn't he come back to get me?*

My feet move against my will, drawing me up the steps. We are only inches apart. A haze of clouded air envelops us, and I want to reach for her. Comfort her. *Who did?*

Her focus shifts to the north. *Tell my mother. I didn't desert her. I was coming back.* Her hand smooths the gown over her abdomen. *When this is over, I'll come home.*

Someone calls my name, but it's far, far away.

The woman looks at me again. *I want to go home. Can you show me the way?*

I feel a tug on my heart. As my mentor and friend Winter has taught me to do, I reach for the image of a lighted doorway to the afterlife. I wait for it to materialize. Usually, it happens as soon as the trapped spirit is ready to move on, or I call it up. Along with seeing ghosts, I can connect them to what lies on the other side.

Nothing happens. No light, no doorway...nothing.

I try again, panic clogging my chest. Why isn't it showing up?

Ava, a voice whispers. A familiar scent teases my nose.

I blink. *Aunt Willa?*

Without conscience thought, I step back from the ghost. She reaches out an ethereal hand. *Don't leave me. Help me.*

I can't allow her to touch me. I know this deep inside with such conviction, I jerk, stumbling down the steps. My ankle twists and I lose my balance.

When I hit the ground, the impact jars the breath from my lungs. The grip of the ghost world is knocked from my awareness. Sprawled on the lawn, I see the grass is green, the roses defying the coming winter in deep reds and yellows.

Moxley sits a few feet away, watching me with a curious tilt of his head. As I sit up, he lumbers over, the tips of his ears dragging along the ground before he sniffs my face and licks my cheek.

I snuggle his thick, warm body tightly, glancing around. The woman is gone and everything appears normal.

"Persephone, I need you." I release the dog and get to my feet, flinching at the pain in my ankle when I put weight on it.

She doesn't appear. No one else does either. Maybe it's better that way. No ghosts attacking me, no friends wondering if I've lost my mind.

I eye the gazebo's foundation. Is there a body buried under it? That might explain her earthbound spirit inside, yet, I've lived here for a year and never encountered her before. I fear there may only be one sure way to find out if her bones are under that section of ground.

Hoofing it to the house, I think of the commotion digging the yard up will entail. Best to put it off for now. Her spirit isn't ready to move on yet, and I already have too many things on my plate to take care of at the moment.

Moxley follows, and once we're inside, I take a quick moment to brush myself off and pour a shot of brandy before I answer Mama's call. My hands shake as I lift the liquor and I set the glass back down. No amount of liquid courage is going to get me through this day.

Through the display window in my office, I see Logan on the sidewalk chatting with Drew and his father, smoothing things over. It's as if no time has passed. As I ease into my chair and put Mama on speakerphone, I massage my ankle. Rosie is on another line, chatting with one of our brides about her Christmas wedding. "Hey, Mama," I say.

"Ava!" Her voice is loud enough that I turn the volume down. "Finally. If I didn't know better, I'd think you were avoiding me."

"I would never do that. I lost my cell and it's been a really-ly..." I detest the word crazy. But sometimes, there's no better way to say it. "Crazy day."

"What's wrong?"

Just everything. "I'm getting married two days from now and I'm a little overwhelmed. Imagine that."

"I know your stressed-out voice, and this isn't it. This is your *I've got a ghost problem* voice."

She knows me well. I chuckle, realizing it's a relief to hear my mother's chiding. She is rock for me in this world, even though she hates the fact I see and speak to the dead.

Aunt Willa, her sister, could, too. "The ghost has to wait. I have too many real-life things to deal with."

There are a few seconds of strained silence, and I can almost hear her nod when she says, "Good. They *should*. This is your special weekend, and they don't get to intrude on it. Have you practiced your speech?"

In Thornhollow, there isn't much that's more important than community. A little old thing like getting married, even if it is to Helen Cross' son, takes second place to giving this five-minute address that is a sacred tradition in our town. Sometimes lying is the easiest way to handle this type of conversation with her, but first, I'll try asking for help. "I was hoping you might do it."

"*Me?*" The drama is real. I can hear the eye roll, as well as the pride I would ask her to do it, in her voice. "Don't be ridiculous. I gave it last year, and the town wants to see their Chamber president in action. Go ahead. Let me hear the first line."

I haven't written the thing, much less practiced it. She's good at off-the-cuff orations. Me, not so much. Yet, under her urging, I feel a surge of defensiveness. "Why?"

"The first and last lines are the most important element of the entire speech, Ava. You know this. Your opening has to hook your listeners. Grab their attention. Let me hear it."

I close my eyes and try to shift into the leader my mother wishes me to be, imagining the gathered tourists and towns-folk lining the sidewalks of Main Street, waiting. My mind is blank, and imagining all those people looking to me for inspiring words causes me to break out in hives. I abandon massaging my ankle and scratch at my arm. "Um, I'm still perfecting it. I'll send it to you later."

"Ava." Wish I had a nickel for every time I heard *that* tone. "Please tell me you have it ready."

"Mama, don't be ridiculous. It is and I will text you the first line later."

"Email me the whole thing. I'll go over it and make some suggestions."

"I appreciate the offer, but honestly, Mama, it's not necessary."

She huffs. "I know you. I also know you've been distracted. Just admit the truth—you haven't even started it. Do you want me to write it for you?"

That would be awesome, but it would also remind me that I'm probably the least unworthy person in town to be chamber president. I'm *always* distracted, but I feel a duty to fill Aunt Willa's shoes. I also hate letting my mother down. "I will email it to you and feel free to add your suggestions," I say around the pit in my stomach. "I'm sorry, but I have to get back to the Cross estate and finish the decorations."

Out on the sidewalk, Drew and Logan shake hands, and Howard nods at my husband before the father and son get in a forest green Jaguar. I take a moment to watch Logan as he waves them off and heads up the walk to the house, a slip of sunlight catching on his wheat-colored hair. As if he feels my gaze, he lifts his head and smiles at me.

"I can stop by tonight and help, if you want," Mama offers. "Your father, too."

I cringe at the thought but force myself to be honest. I need her. "I may take you up on that." Logan enters and crosses to me, dropping a kiss on my forehead. He sets a hip on the edge of the desk, waiting for me to finish. "Let's talk after dinner, okay?"

"Don't worry, Ava. Everything's going to be fine. Love you."

I pray she's right. "Love you, too, Mama."

I disconnect and accept Logan's hand when he extends it. "You look exhausted." He frowns down at me. "You'd be better off to go upstairs and take a nap than to run out to the vineyard. I can cancel the bachelor party and take over the reception stuff."

I squeeze his hand and rise. "I can handle it, but if you want to write my speech for the parade tomorrow night, I wouldn't stop you."

He draws me into a hug. "I'll have something outlined for you before dinner. Sound good?"

I rest my head on his shoulder. "What would I do without you?"

Moxley gives a woof and we break apart. Logan pushes off the desk and pets the dog. "Is Kit all right?"

I'm not sure. "She doesn't want to talk about whatever happened between her and Dr. Hurley. All I know is that his wife was trying to kill him, and Kit warned him about her."

He whistles under his breath. "He knows Kit's psychic?"

"I don't think it mattered then. Things didn't end well. What is this about a teaching gig?"

Across the foyer, Rosie hangs up and takes a second call.

Logan fiddles with his tie. "Abbey is going on maternity leave in April and they need someone to fill in for her until finals. It's only seven weeks, unless the baby comes early."

Dr. Abbey Rhodes is our age and one of the school's elite graduates. "You enjoyed subbing for her before, but it was only a week. Are you prepared for that much? That's a long time to be away from your practice." *And me.*

"She only has two classes next semester that meet on

Tuesdays and Thursdays, and there's an online study group she hosts once a month. She'll grade the finals, so I won't have to. It wouldn't be all that much."

"Her Type A personality is going to get a surprise when that baby comes," I tell him.

He gives me a crooked grin. "Are you psychic now, too?"

"I've seen what Rosie and Jenn have dealt with since the arrival of their new additions. Rosie is an experienced mom, and Avalene is still challenging her daily."

"Sounds a lot like her godmother."

I poke him. I love that little girl as if she's my own. "Watch it, or you'll sound like Persephone."

He grabs my hand and leads me toward the kitchen. "When was the last time you ate?"

"I had a brownie half an hour ago."

A funny look passes over his face. "Half an hour ago we were at Gloria's picking up your dress."

I check the clock. He's right. I'm losing track of time. I rub my forehead. "Guess it was only a few minutes ago. Seems longer."

He sits me at the table and starts pulling out stuff from the fridge to build a sandwich. "I don't want my bride passing out on me before she even gets down the aisle."

Since I'm usually the one taking care of others, it's nice to allow him to take care of me. "I have to finish the decorations in the barn, write my speech and send it to Mama, and then I'm going to fall into bed and sleep until sunrise tomorrow."

"I think I should skip the bachelor party."

He slides a plate with a chicken salad sandwich cut in half in front of me. I dive into a section, speaking around a mouthful. Mama would kill me for my bad manners. "Absolutely not. You're the whole reason for it to begin with. You deserve to have some fun with your friends and brother. You know me, I'll be fine. Mama and Daddy are coming over and I'll pawn a few errands on them."

Logan doesn't look convinced, but he nods before resting a hand on my shoulder. "You'll call me if you need anything, promise?"

"I promise," I say, wiping crumbs from my chin. "This is really good. Thank you."

He kisses me and heads to his office for a video conference with an elderly client who has trouble leaving the house. He'd suggested earlier that he could cancel it so we could finish some last-minute email invitations to a few more friends St. Helen decided to invite. I'd insisted he be here to talk to Mrs. Sparten, an eighth-year-old woman who recently became widowed and has been leaning on him for advice concerning her husband's estate.

I'm starting on the second half of my late lunch when Kit bursts through the back. "I can't take it. I have to go."

I hurriedly stand and follow her to the front foyer, swallowing and wiping my hands on my napkin. "Go where?"

"Anywhere away from here."

She's out the door and down the steps before I can call after her. Standing on the front porch, I watch as she races off, crossing through the tea shop's side yard and disappearing down the alley behind it.

Sage emerges and peers at me across the road. Rosie joins me on the top step. "What was that all about?" she asks. "I swear, she needs to see a therapist."

If only that would help.

Sage leans over her railing, peering down the alley, before she calls, "Is everything okay?"

"No," I reply. "What's new?"

She gives a knowing smile. "Should I go after her? I can close early."

I think about going after Kit, too. "Maybe it's better if we give her some space. If you have time, can you come for dinner tonight?"

She doesn't even hesitate. "Does seven work?"

"Yes. See you then."

Behind us, Rosie's phone rings, and she hurries inside to answer it. A moment later, as I'm shutting the door and trying to figure out what to do about my friend, the weird ghost stuff, and the opening line for my speech, she informs me, "Jenn needs you. Mrs. Cross is insisting on rearranging the bridal and parent tables."

Of course, she is. I lean against the door and gaze up at the heavens. "Did I do something in a past life to deserve this?"

"Past life?" Persephone is suddenly standing in front of me, decked in a kaftan with lemon yellow and purple roses all over it. Her earrings match, and her necklace is a giant peacock that hangs around her belly button.

Rosie can't see her, but the cats can and they hiss and run away. *Do guardian angels have belly buttons?*

Now I'm sure I'm losing it from all the stress. I lower my voice. "I called you twenty minutes ago."

She grunts, returning to my earlier statement. "Maybe you should ask if it's something you've done in *this* lifetime."

"I've done a lot of good," I mumble, then to Rosie, "Tell Jenn I'll be there in fifteen."

She returns to the phone and Persephone shakes her head. "You need to cancel the reception."

"Are you kidding me?" My voice comes out too loud, and I catch Rosie shooting me a quizzical look as she hangs up.

"Is there a ghost in here?" she asks.

"No," I tell her, shoving away and going into my office to grab my purse. "But there is a pain in my—"

"Hey!" Persephone wags a finger at me. "Careful, or I'll leave you to the ghosts."

There are moments, like the one earlier, when I feel as if she already has.

FIVE

"You don't have to be so mean, you know," she chastises as she trails after me. "You should appreciate me more."

Spirit guides and guardian angels—she's both—are not all they're cracked up to be. At least, mine isn't. I wave at Rosie. "I'll be at the vineyard."

"Find your cell while you're there," she calls.

In the car, Persephone takes the passenger seat like a flesh-and-blood human. "You need to make Samuel cross over."

"Of all the things I need help with, that's what you're advising me to focus on? I promised he could stay until after the ceremony, and I intend to keep that promise."

"This wedding is a farce. You're already married."

I bite my lip. Houses and shops lining the streets are done in fall colors, yellow, orange, and red mums everywhere. The town square has an antique wagon filled with hay bales and huge pumpkins in it. Families are getting photos of their young children posed on the bales, caramel apples on sticks in hand. "What did Sherlock do now to upset you?"

She turns her face to the window. "I don't know what you're talking about."

"You're only down on weddings when you're fighting with him."

"He's terrible at relationships."

There's the pot calling the ghostly kettle black. We hit the highway heading north and the elevated hills where grapevines grow. "You might take a look in the mirror."

"What?"

"How many romantic relationships have you had?"

Her hesitation tells me she's trying to find a way to lie or divert the conversation since she's never had a boyfriend and we both know it. "He doesn't understand me." She flicks her gaze my way. "And he's bossy. Just like you."

Again, pot, kettle. "You and I have different opinions regarding your role in my life. I've never been a spirit guide and you've never been human. It's challenging for each of us to understand the other's perspective. Perhaps it's the same with you and Sherlock over the nature of your romance."

She's quiet for a long time. I have questions to ask, but the silence is actually nice, and when she's in a mood like this, she won't give good advice anyway.

The silence ends when I make the turn for the estate. The drive to the house is long and dotted with cars and delivery vans. She leans against the headrest and closes her eyes. "I'm not cut out for this."

"Having a romantic partner or being my guide?"

"Both."

I don't disagree. In the beginning, I'd hoped she was going to be a resource for me with my ghost troubles. To some extent, she has been, but the rules are the rules. She can't flat out tell me what to do. Free will and all that.

I'm not the best cheerleader, and it's discomforting to admit I need her, but I am compelled to get her back on track. "Don't quit on me now."

The decorations in town pale to those here. The entire forty-acre estate is one giant autumn extravaganza. Even the trellises in the fields sport colorful fall leaf garlands. I pull in near the barn and see Helen and Jenn arguing through the open double doors. "Besides, you've helped me and quite a few earthbound spirits in the past year. You should focus on your successes." I swear, I sound like Mama.

Lia rushes from the barn with a relieved smile, waving enthusiastically. Persephone sighs. "I'll help you with your speech."

I shut off the car and pocket my keys. "For the festival? Why would you do that?"

"Not the festival." Sherlock materializes in the back seat, startling us. He locks eyes with me in the rearview. "The one you're going to need to convince your grandparents that Samuel can't hang around any longer."

Persephone whirls. "Were you eavesdropping?"

I glance between them. "Samuel has already agreed to move on after he sees me walk down the aisle."

Persephone gives me a stern look. "You really are gullible. After all the fun Tabitha and Samuel have enjoyed since being reunited, you believe he'll go willingly?"

"He can visit her any time, just like Sherlock does you."

She shakes her head. "They've both defied the natural order of things. He was trapped for three hundred years in that time capsule. She's been using magic to stay in her physical body. It's causing a time-space continuum issue."

"Is that why the grid is gummed up?"

"What are you talking about?"

Lia reaches us and opens my door. "Are you talking to yourself or a ghost? Can I get my stuff and record it?"

"No." It comes out gruff and I soften my voice. "No ghost hunting today, please."

Persephone chuckles. "Too late for that."

"Lia?" Again, I hear my mother in my tone. I leave my purse behind as I climb out. "Have you been helping Jenn decorate, or trying to record ghosts?"

She giggles. "Busted." She glances at the arguing women in the barn. "I might've gotten sidetracked from the decorating."

"Great." The argument gains volume and velocity. I take a deep breath and prep myself to face my mother-in-law. "If any of your equipment is in plain sight, put it in Jenn's van right now and then sit on the veranda until I call you."

"It's not out, I swear. I was simply talking to any spirits who might be around."

"But you can't hear them answer you."

Her eyes light up. "I asked one to move a fork. Not only did he—or maybe she—do it, they threw it across the room! It hit Mrs. Cross in the butt!"

Persephone laughs. I gape. "It did *what?*" This is bad. No wonder Helen is livid. "I thought Jenn called because Helen wanted to rearrange tables."

"She did and she does. But the argument sort of escalated after the fork incident. Mrs. Cross thinks Jenn threw it."

As Mama always proclaims, the only way to eat an elephant is one bite at a time. This is one big elephant.

First, I need to intervene between Helen and Jenn. Once

I have them cooled down, I'll speak to Persephone and Sherlock about my grandparents and their future. I lean down and address them, still in the vehicle. "We'll continue our discussion as soon as I'm done here. I want your word, Persephone, that you will be available when I call for you."

She sticks out her tongue and disappears.

Classy, as always.

Sherlock looks slightly abashed. "I hear you misplaced your handheld phone. Would you like me to look for it?"

"That would be awesome." At least he's helpful. "Thank you."

I march toward the women. "Ladies, we're all under a lot of pressure, and I assure you, everything's going to be fine." Together, they turn toward me and start complaining, raising their voices over the other as they meet me in the yard. I hold up a hand to my mother-in-law. "Helen, your request to rearrange the tables is doable. Jenn and I will adjust our layout and you can help us with shifting the decorations. We don't have time for a major overhaul of the entire barn, however. You can start by removing the centerpieces, then the place settings." Helen sucks in a breath, and I cut her off before she can argue. "Jenn did not throw a fork at you; a ghost did, so please stop blaming her."

Her mouth falls open for a split second, then snaps shut.

Jenn gives a smug smile. "Told you I didn't do it."

Helen ignores her, eyes shooting daggers my way. "You weren't even here, Ava."

At least she's come to accept that I'm a ghost whisperer. The idea doesn't sit well, but since I broke a family curse for her last year, and she's seen me in action, she's wrestled with her misgivings and stopped denying it.

"A ghost told me." I feel slightly guilty about lying, but

it's better than dragging Lia into it. Unfortunately, the cognizant spectral beings watching this confrontation are offended. One, a forty-ish man in a striped suit and dark hat, shakes his head in disgust—he's probably strong enough to manipulate matter and cause the fork to fly through the air. With a threatening glare, he goes back to his card game with the other spirits around him. Helen would no doubt die of heart failure if she saw them doing that over the Havilland.

"Oh," she says, tugging on the hem of her wool jacket. "I didn't realize."

Jenn appears vindicated. She's not happy about the table situation, though. "You should put on some old clothes. Wouldn't want your designer threads to get dirty, and believe me, this is dirty work."

Helen doesn't shy from physical labor—if it serves her goals. Rearranging the heavy tables, though, gives her pause. "I'll have Leonard assist." He's the overseer of the farm, a hard worker who is usually between the rows of grapevines. Since the harvest is done for this season, he's no doubt in his office on the other side of the property, planning for next year's crop. "Mr. Cross can help, too."

It amuses me when she refers to her husband in that manner, but as Mama often says, she's as southern as cornbread. "Isn't he attending the bachelor party?" I ask.

"The golfing, yes. Not the rest."

"Well, we'll need you to tackle the place settings."

She gives me a stern frown. "Can't Lia handle them?"

"You're okay entrusting her with your grandmother's fine china?"

The frown deepens. She turns on her heel and leaves.

Jenn and I exchange a look and she shrugs. "Sorry, boss. I

tried to be patient and professional, like you always preach, but nothing I say or do makes that woman happy."

"You are not alone in that," I murmur. "For everyone's sake, let's make the best of it." We tromp after the matriarch.

Inside, Helen is studying the north end of the structure which we've decorated with flowering plants, flowing fabric hanging from the rafters, and oodles of white twinkle lights. Our colors are royal blue and gold, and a lovely marble wishing well has been placed to the right of the long, rectangular wedding party table. It's something new we've been marketing to brides, and using at other events as well. Who doesn't love the fun of making a wish?

To our left is the round table for our immediate family members. Helen shifts her eyes to that and I see the wheels spinning. She rarely, if ever, isn't in the spotlight, and although it's mine and Logan's day, this whole elaborate reception is for her.

"If we move the bridal party here," she says, motioning at the expanse, "we can open the side doors and enjoy the backdrop of the hills with the sun setting. Presentation is everything, Ava."

It's actually a great idea, and I wonder why I didn't think of it myself. "You're right. It will be breathtaking. Problem is, we won't see it if it's behind us." I walk to the place I'll be sitting next to Logan. "From here, though, I'll have a perfect view."

"It will be easier for the photographer to capture the candid shots," Jenn offers. "He won't be fighting the sun in the background."

"That's true." I go to the double doors, once used as entry to the speakeasy, and later for horse riders. With both open, I draw in a deep breath, surveying the landscape. It's late afternoon and the sun is low on the horizon, just like it will be on Saturday. "But it would be a lovely backdrop for the wishing well."

Jenn snaps her fingers, catching on to my strategy. "The family seating would be closer to your table, and that would be better for pictures, too."

"You'll have a full view of the party guests, dance floor, and the well," I add to Helen. *And everyone will be able to see you.*

My mother-in-law's frown disappears. I meet Jenn's eyes and we hold our collective breaths, waiting for her to respond.

She offers a thoughtful nod. "Very well. That will work."

Which means we only have to move the family table and wishing well. While the well appears to be one hundred percent white and gray marble, it's actually a lightweight aluminum underneath the coating and it has hidden wheels. Since it's not filled with water yet, the three of us can scoot it across the concrete floor easily.

In minutes, we've swapped the table for it and Helen and Jenn work on replacing the plates and silverware, while I move several pots of ferns and trailing ivy around the well. Once finished, we stand back and analyze our progress. The setting sun shoots fiery orange layers through the pale blue sky and lingering gray clouds.

"I hope it doesn't rain," Helen says.

"The weatherman is calling for blue skies," Jenn reassures her. I'm not sure that's true, but positive thinking never hurts.

Lia peeks her head in. "Wow."

"I told you to stay on the patio." I brush my hands

together and tweak a string of lights around the DJ's setup. "What are you doing here?"

"It's been twenty minutes. I was afraid you killed each other."

I tell Jenn to take her home, and they say goodbye to Helen. She stands and watches them go before studying the interior. "Was it truly a ghost that threw that fork at me?"

The suspected culprit now lurks near the punch bowl. If I let myself tune into him and the ghostly layer that clings to this place, I can almost hear the strains of jazz music, and see flapper girls on my dance floor. The phantom man raises a glass of dark liquor, grinning at Helen before he shoots it back.

"Yes," I tell her. "And we need to send him to the other side so he doesn't cause trouble at the reception."

She arches a brow and glances around, trying to see who I'm talking about. "He?"

I glare at the spirit, but he ignores me, his focus solely on my mother-in-law. I don't like the gleam in his eyes. "I've already tried to clear this place with every technique I know. I think I'm going to have to pick something a bit stronger. Force the issue."

"I've never noticed any of them being malicious before."

"I'm not sure why they are now, but it may be because this is so important to you. You're generating a lot of energy and stirring them up."

She heaves a heavy sigh and links her hands in front of her. I've seen her do this before when she's stressed and trying not to show it. "I'm glad we have a moment alone. Logan is special. I love Chuck, don't get me wrong, and I've never played favorites, but Logan? He is the future of Cross Enterprises."

I bet if Logan was here, he would reject the idea that she's pinning the business on his shoulders. "Chuck seems like the more obvious choice to take over."

Logan's brother runs a brewery a few towns over and has plenty of business sense, even if he's not great with his personal relationships.

"He will never have a family. The winery and our other business investments should go to my offspring."

The pointed look she gives me makes me want to tuck tail and run. I've already been asked by at least a dozen people when Logan and I are going to start a family. Helen hasn't been so rude as to come out and directly ask, but there have been hints, like this one. "Have you discussed your legacy with Logan?" It's the only thing I can think to ask. While it's true that after being around Rosie and Jenn's babies this summer, I have felt the urge to have one of my own, I rather like my life right now. Adding a baby to the mix might be too much. I want to enjoy my husband a while longer before we introduce another Cross into the world. I want to be a good mom, and that means feeling satisfied with where I am.

"I've been prepping him to take over since he was born."

Sherlock appears and gestures toward the house. "I found your phone. You might have difficulty getting it back, though."

Great. I need to get away from Helen. Getting into the house without her, though, could be a problem. "I need to head back. Could I use your bathroom before I go?"

"Of course," she says, and motions me to go ahead, while she closes up the barn.

As I hustle across the lawn toward the looming mansion, decorated as beautifully as the barn in anticipation of the wedding and reception, I quiz him. "Is it in a toilet or something?"

"No, not that."

"What is it then?"

Inside, I pause as a hush falls. The butler is nowhere to be seen, and I follow Sherlock as he guides me to the rear of the first floor. A faint humming meets my ears and draws me deeper into a small room off the kitchen. It appears to be deserted, once used by servants who lived here, but now filled with dust and cobwebs. A female ghost, dressed as a maid, glances up from the sewing in her lap. "Oh, hello. Your friend said you were looking for me."

On the table beside her, stacks of books and an oil lamp compete for space with a set of keys, some coins, a hairbrush, and a single earring. Next to this oddball collection lies my cell. And to top it off, an old revolver.

I point at my phone. "I believe that belongs to me."

She shields it with a hand and smiles pleasantly, but there's something unnerving in her eyes. "Not anymore."

SIX

"A bit of a kleptomaniac, I'm afraid," Sherlock tells me. "She's amassed quite a collection through the years."

I glance around the small room, taking it in this time. Every surface is covered with random trinkets, each piece of furniture strewn with clothes. "You worked here?"

"Still do," she says with a lift of her chin.

Does she not realize she's dead? Some don't. I normally ease them into the idea, but today, I don't have the time or patience. "Sorry, but you don't any longer. How did you die?"

Her face goes as white as my bridal gown. "What?"

"You expired," Sherlock says. "Croaked. Kicked the bucket. You're a ghost, stuck here due to some unresolved issue, most likely surrounding your death. Tell her how it happened. She can help you move on."

She comes out of the chair, blustering. The sewing falls to the floor. "I'm no ghost! I'm waiting for my daughter. She'll be back any time now."

What are the odds? If she's collected so many things, she's strong. Her tie to a loved one could be the reason. "Where did she go?"

"I...she..." She shakes her head, seeming confused, then turns from us and glides across the floor to a shelf near a single bed. On it is a sepia-toned picture of a young girl. A candle, a prayer card with Mother Mary, and a cross necklace are centered there. "She's coming back," the woman insists.

A part of me simply wants to snatch my phone and leave. Another knows I need to help this woman. "What's your name?"

"Nettie." She keeps her gaze pinned on the photograph. "Nettie Mars."

Before I join her at the shrine to her daughter, I swipe my phone, pocketing it. "Is that her?"

A tremulous smile crosses her face. She reaches out to touch the dusty picture, her hand going through it. She pulls it back, worrying her hands in front of her. "That's her. My Maria Grace. I light a candle for her every night. It will help her find her way back to me."

In the photo, Maria Grace looks to be about eight. A quick calculation tells me it's possible she could still be alive. "How old is she?"

"Nineteen." Nettie nods. "Such a bright girl. She has a wonderful future ahead of her if she can just get away from here. From him."

"Who?"

The smile disappears, and she shakes her head this time, pacing to the bed. "He promised to make a respectable woman out of her, but I know his kind. See them all the time down at the joint. They come and go, seducing innocent young women and discarding them when they've had their fill. My Maria Grace knows better. She'll be back once she sees him for who he is."

My mind flashes to the young woman in the gazebo. "How long has it been since you've seen her?"

Nettie whirls, the limp fabric of her skirt flaring at her ankles. "Just yesterday. Or... It's been a week or two." She rubs at her temple. "I keep losing track of time."

You and me, both, sister.

"Because, as we've said," Sherlock tells her, "you're no longer alive."

A fierceness takes over her features, and she snarls at him. "You're lying. I want you to leave now." She glances from him to me. "Both of you. Get out!"

I debate whether staying is in my best interest. I've crossed paths with certain spirits who are strong like her and the fork-thrower in the barn. Hanging onto the earthly plane, they gather energy. That unnerving gleam is in her eyes again, and I'm pretty sure I don't want to see what she can accomplish when she's angry. "Who is the man she left with? Can you tell me his name? I can find him and bring her home."

Trying to hang onto her anger, but hope forcing it away, she hesitates, then says, "Robert Ventura. Goes by Bobby V. He's a bootlegger. A two-time hustler and thief."

My mouth falls open. "Bobby The Phantom Ventura?"

Her face scrunches in disgust. "I see you've heard of him. Figures. Your kind sticks together, don't you?"

"What kind is that?" I ask, knowing what she means but annoyed just the same.

"Sinners. Malcontents. Think you're better than the rest of us."

Sherlock rolls his eyes. I let it go. While not as infamous as Al Capone, Dillinger, or Bonnie and Clyde, Ventura was a local who won the hearts of many because he destroyed mortgage notes at the banks he robbed, and regularly dropped off large sums of money at orphanages and churches. He gained enough celebrity status that we learned about him in school.

Ignoring the fact she has a bit of thievery going on herself, I also try to suppress a grin. Ventura was definitely on the wrong side of the law, yet he was a hero in these parts. He'd been left at the police station on the steps as a toddler and they'd had little choice but to send him to St. Mary's Orphanage, long ago closed and eventually torn down. On that site now stood our funeral parlor. Ventura had never been adopted, but legends claimed he took on the older brother role to kids throughout his time there, and when he bugged out at fifteen, made sure the nuns had a stockpile of goods "donated" to them. It was suspected he'd stolen all of it from wealthy folks and various politicians who'd attempted to close the place over the years. A Robin Hood character, it was tough to dislike him. "You're sure? Bobby V?"

"You don't think I know who he is? My daughter has a good heart," she assures me in a defensive tone. "He's tricked her into believing he loves her."

I scan my memory for any reference we might have read in school about a woman in the gangster's life. History wasn't my best subject. "You're positive she left with him?"

"Yes, I'm positive. Why else would she leave?"

"She ran away," Sherlock says in his usual cut-and-dried manner. He isn't much for emotional claims and prefers facts. "Sounds like a healthy young woman. Did you expect her to stay here"—he flips a hand around at the room—"and be a maid like you?"

She bristles. "You have no right to—"

My phone rings, cutting her off. It's my best friend, Brax. "Hey," he says when I answer. Sherlock and Nettie continue arguing but only I can hear them. I shush them with a hand over the speaker as he continues. "What did you do?"

"Sorry?"

"We have a problem." He sounds as if he's about to tear down the walls. "A big one."

They seem to be stacking up. What's another to add to my list? "I'm heading home. Can it wait until I get there?"

"Afraid not. Swing by The Toad."

Brax and Rhys own The Thorny Toad Bar and Grill. It doubles as a metaphysical hangout for those into psychic readings, chakra healing, and sound therapy. "Why? What's up?"

"Kit is leaving."

Kit rents a booth and gives readings on the weekends as Madam X, a stage name. She's so incredibly accurate, she's booked months in advance. "She needs a break," I tell him. "A few days off. That's all."

"She's not taking time off, she's *leaving town*. When I asked why, she said, 'Ask Ava. She's the reason.' What did you do?"

At that moment, the door flies open and Winston stands there. "What on earth are you doing in here?"

"Found my missing phone," I say, waving it at him and forcing him out of the way as I brush past. To Brax, I ask, "Is she still there?"

"Not for long."

"Don't let her leave." There's nothing I can do for Nettie at the moment and I have more pressing matters to handle. "I'm on my way."

SEVEN

Kit is speeding away in her car as I arrive. Rhys and Braxton are in front of the old, rambling Victorian house they converted into the bar. The evening crowd is getting an early start, flooding the lot and loitering on the sidewalk.

I park around the back and walk to the entrance. Rhys is on the veranda, waiting. He's wearing one of the Toad's signature T-shirts displaying a cartoon toad with a swami hat sitting on an Ouija board. He holds out a sheet of paper to me. His pale blond hair sticks up in tufts, suggesting he's been raking his fingers through it in distress. "She packed all her stuff and left us with two months' worth of appointments to cancel. What are we going to do?"

Brax, towering over both of us, takes the paper and shoves it in my hand. "Looks like Ava has a new job."

"Oh no." I peer at the dates and corresponding names. "I'm no psychic."

"You can speak to the dead." Brax looks down his nose at me. "Good enough."

Rhys pats his massive bicep. "She's getting married this weekend. She can't help."

My best friend knows very well what's on my agenda. He's standing up with me in place of a traditional maid of honor. He's upset with Kit for bailing on the most profitable weekend of the year, but the irritation in his eyes makes me keep my sarcasm locked up. "I'll talk to her and get this straightened out."

Rhys nearly vibrates with anxiety. "What did you do to set her off?"

As a party of three passes us, I motion the two men to follow me to a quieter corner of the porch and then give them a brief explanation about the magical grid and the blocked energies. "It's messing with her head," I explain. "Causing her third eye to freak out. She was trying to clear it but didn't have any luck. She must figure getting out of town is her only option to relieve the pressure."

Rhys worries his crystal bracelet. "Will she come back if the grid is still blocked?"

"No," Brax answers before I can. "How do we clear it?"

"I'm not sure, but I'm having dinner with Sage. She'll have some ideas."

A couple exits and calls goodbye to my friends. They wave and Rhys tells them to come back soon. Then the smile falls off his face as he returns his attention to me. "Can't your spirit guide help?"

"Tabitha can surely do something," Brax adds.

You would think so, but if she's the reason for the wonky magic, due to the fact she doesn't want to send my grandfather to the afterlife, I doubt she'll volunteer.

A young woman with big, round glasses leans out to call

to us. "Getting crazy in here, guys. Could use more hands on deck."

"Be right there." Rhys gives me a quick hug. "Gotta run. Between here and the B&B we are swamped. Keep us updated, and if you want her booth, it's yours."

"No, thanks, but I'll find some way to help you." I watch him head in, wishing not for the first time I'd insisted on holding the ceremony and reception on a different weekend. I wish I could spend the evening assisting him and Rhys, writing my speech, and enjoying the festivities.

"Call as soon as you have a way to help Kit," Brax says, and he, too, disappears inside.

On my way home, I stop at The Beehive Diner and pick up several of the daily specials—chicken pot pies and a spinach quiche—and check in with Queenie, the owner. "The Toad is hopping," I tell her, as I pay for the food after waiting in line. "Pun intended."

She grins, handing me my change. "My boys are excellent businessmen."

"We good for Saturday?"

She touches the bright swatch of material holding up her textured hair and blows out a tired breath. Her dark eyes dart past me, checking for eavesdroppers and she lowers her voice. "You know who is driving me straight to the nut house, but if you're speaking about the food, everything is peachy. Never thought she'd go for a classic, southern dinner, but it sure makes things easier." Her voice has that soft but comforting accent that I love. She and my mother were best friends growing up, and Brax and I enjoy the same bond. Even after all these years, Mama and Queenie are as tight as sisters, and Brax and I are equally as close. She rubs her wrist as if it's aching. "Good thing I called in Luanna and Marcy to help with all the canapés."

"Is your tendinitis bugging you again?"

"Doc says it's arthritis, and he's prescribed some expensive medication. Squeezing the pastry bag to make 1200 canapés would make anyone sore."

"Good lord." I hadn't thought about that. "Does the medication help?"

"Wouldn't know. I'm using my own blend, all natural." She waves me off. "Now, don't you be telling on me to Brax, y'hear? I'll be fine."

I take the pies and make a zipped-lip motion. "I feel guilty you're wrecking yourself for me."

Queenie rolls her eyes. "You just worry about walking down that aisle and making us all proud."

I hug her over the counter. When I arrive home, I discover Sage already inside, waiting. The kitchen smells like her—a combination of patchouli, lavender, and something else I don't know. Her hair is tucked up on one side and held by a comb with a pentagram on it. I set the bag on the table and flop into a chair. "Some days I can't believe my life."

She chuckles and pulls out the food, taking the slice of quiche for herself and setting one of the mini pies on a plate for me. "You have a pretty awesome one, yet I detect a note of desperation in your voice."

I give her a rundown of the afternoon's events around bites of the creamy chicken and veggies wrapped in flaky crust. Arthur and Lancelot join us, curling around my ankles in hopes I'll share, and Moxley settles on the back door rug. No Tabby, though, in either of her forms. I share my suspicions about the cause of the psychic grid blockage, as well as the possible dead woman buried under the gazebo. "Now

Kit's bailed, I have to cross my grandfather before the pressure gets worse and a horde of angry ghosts breaks through the barrier and descends on this place, and I'm concerned the spirits haunting the speakeasy are going to ruin my reception." I chug the tea Sage made me. It's raspberry, my favorite. "Oh, and Queenie has arthritis in her wrist. Do you have any salve that might help? She claims she's using her personal home blend, but I don't think it's working."

Sage blinks several times and swallows, seeming to digest my litany of problems along with her dinner. "I'll take her my comfrey and sweet fir bee balm. Did you try calling Kit?"

I nod. "Goes straight to voicemail."

"Persephone thinks your grandparents are screwing up the grid but Kit didn't pick up on that?"

I shrug. "She didn't seem to know what was causing it."

"And you haven't felt it?"

"I'm not psychic."

She finishes her last bite. "Not all psychics are mediums, but all mediums are psychic."

I wish I was neither. "I've been consumed with the wedding and Fall Festival activities. Have *you* sensed anything?"

"Nothing, and as intense as it seems to be affecting Kit, you'd think one of us would have noticed it."

She might, but I'm not tuned in to that stuff like she is, regardless of what she claims about my abilities. I place the extra pot pies in the fridge for the next day. Logan loves Queenie's cooking as much as I do and neither of us has time for making meals right now. "Let's walk outside. I want to see if that young woman will talk to me again."

The sinking sun teases us, thin fingers reaching through the tree leaves, throwing bars of peach and pink over our faces. The frogs and crickets are already warming up, long shadows spreading quickly on these shorter fall days.

"Do you see a group of ghosts around the property right now?" Sage asks.

"I only noticed them when I experienced that first..." I struggle to find the best term for it. "Episode. Do you?"

"No, but I feel one. Seems old and shy."

Sounds like the man who peeked around the corner of the house this afternoon. "That's good, isn't it? That the angry mob is gone?"

She idles near the gazebo, eyes sharp and observant. "I suppose. And the second episode? Did you notice any then?"

"Just the pregnant gal."

"Hmm."

The simple reply sends a chill over me. Or maybe it's the cool night air creeping in. "What are you thinking?"

She removes her shoes and strolls barefoot down the hill a ways, toward the farmhouse, but halts when Tabitha emerges from the front door, staring at us in her human form. Her face is serene but in shadow, and I can't see her green eyes.

"I sense a nexus," Sage says quietly, once she's returned, "but there's no blockage. No collection of earthbound spirits or dammed-up energy. The grid is a network, each thread connected to the others. There is a higher wattage here, but it's coming from your grandmother, not Samuel or any blocked magic."

Speak of the devil. Samuel joins Tabitha, seeming to become more corporeal as he wraps his arms around her waist. She tilts her head, exposing her neck for him to kiss and allowing him to draw energy from her via the contact. "Are ye needin' us?" she calls.

I shake my head. *Nothing to see here, folks.* Then I face Sage and keep my voice low. "So what's hurting Kit, if it's not wonky magic? Keeping Samuel here isn't the cause?"

"I don't believe so." Her gaze follows some invisible line I can't detect from the gazebo down to the willow tree at the creek and back to my house. "Your wards are intact and there's no unusual activity I can detect."

"Persephone's wrong?" I snort. "That makes my day in more ways than one. But what *is* causing Kit's problem?"

"I think she's under psychic attack." She meets my eyes. "You may be, too."

"Me?" I draw back, rubbing my arms against the cold air. "Who would do such a thing?"

"Only a very powerful psychic could get past Kit's defenses and cause her so much pain and confusion. And only a stupid one would cross your grandmother by causing you to hallucinate ghosts on top of it."

"Hallucinate?"

She retrieves her shoes and we stroll to the back porch. "They may be by-products of what's happening with Kit."

"How so?"

She pauses, searching for a way to explain. "Sort of a leaking of the spell and you're soaking it up. It could also be directed at you, and she's being affected by it."

"But I don't know any psychics besides you and her."

She holds the screen door open for me. "And Tabitha."

Inside, I lean on the countertop and rub the spot between my brows, which aches from mental overload. "She's more witch than anything else. Besides, she wouldn't harm either of us. Could it be a vendor at The Thorny Toad? Maybe they're mad at Kit for sucking up all their customers."

Sage slips on her shoes. "I know most of them and none are strong enough to pull off this level of assault."

"How can we help her?"

She grabs her bag from the kitchen chair. "First we have to find her, and then,"—she turns and gives me a grim look—"we're going to need Raven and her favorite athame."

"A knife?" My voice comes out in a screech that sends my cats scrambling from their sleeping places and Moxley to raise both ears. "For what?"

"To cut out whatever magical worm has invaded her brain."

EIGHT

Sunrise is only minutes away the next morning when I slip out of bed.

Last night, Logan came home earlier than I'd expected and is now lying on his stomach, snoring softly. Mama and Daddy stopped by and I sent them to the church with the pew decorations. Around ten, Brax and Rhys came over to discuss Kit and I'd brought them and Logan up-to-date on Sage's theory.

I check my phone as I go downstairs, avoiding the one creaky step so I won't wake my husband, and hoping Moxley's nails don't give us away as he follows. There are no messages from Kit and I asked my dad last night to put out feelers for her with his buddies on the police force. Our current chief wouldn't do anything official since she's left on her own accord and Detective Jones doesn't put stock in magic.

I want to take a moment to marvel at my dress, hanging in a spare room, since I didn't have a chance the previous day, but first I need coffee.

Arthur and Lancelot are waiting by their dishes as the automatic coffee maker clicks on and begins brewing. I inhale the fresh scent and draw my robe's ties a little closer. These quiet, early mornings are a balm to my heart. It's my form of meditation. Of soaking in how good my life is.

Today is the official kickoff of the festival, and lucky for me, Logan whipped up a decent speech before bed last night. After tweaking it, I sent it to Mama as requested and took her return suggestions in stride, adding a few of them to make her happy. I will give the short but sweet address at three to start the parade, and I've designated Baylor to ride in the procession in my place so I can bug out and finish reception preparations.

After feeding the cats and Mox, I take my mug to the back porch and enjoy watching the sun push through the last vestiges of the night. The dog plops down next to my feet and makes a slight sighing noise, seeming as content to view the dawning of a new day as I am. It has become our routine, a few minutes of peace before the chaos kicks in.

Scanning the grounds, I pause at the gazebo. Nothing seems amiss. No pregnant woman, no bleached-out landscape, no crowd of angry spirits. The elderly gentleman from the previous day peeks at me from the hedge between us and the B&B but I'm not ghost-whispering this early. Besides, he seems harmless and rather timid, disappearing as soon as I catch his eye. I'd be better off sending Sherlock to discover why he's hanging around and how he's gotten past my wards. Then I can send him to the afterlife next week when things have settled down.

A cardinal trills and a light breeze ripples the leaves, a few cascading to the ground while we watch. A squirrel darts down a tree trunk and races into the nearest flower bed, shaking a few and causing their petals to drop in a feathery shower of reds and golds.

"I hope you're proud of how this place is doing," I murmur to my Aunt Willa. It's hard to believe how much my life has changed since her death. "And that you'll be at the ceremony on Saturday, watching over me."

The squirrel emerges and chitters, before running back to his tree. On the way, he bumps into a rose bush and the largest of the flowers waves back and forth. I wait to smell my aunt's perfume or feel the tell-tale breeze that always accompanies her visits, but neither comes.

Disappointed, I reassure myself the rose is a sign, a confirmation, yet it feels like a lie. I miss Aunt Willa terribly and her absence feels especially keen now. Seeing her spirit has alluded me time and time again. Everyone else's, no problem. A twisted irony.

Inside, I refill my cup. My phone dings with a message from Sage, dragging me from my thoughts. *Did you find her?*

I send a thumbs-down emoji.

I'll use my dousing pendulum.

This time, I give her a thumbs up.

I'm heading upstairs to look at my dress when my phone rings. Logan is at the top, stretching and yawning. He offers me a crooked smile, and I return a grin. Even with his bedhead and in his pjs, he's handsome.

I figure it's Mama since she often calls at the crack of dawn, but Sage's name shows on the screen. Logan shuffles down the stairs and I hand him the cup as I answer. "That was fast. Did you find her already?"

"Yes."

He sips, then kisses me, handing it back. "Everything okay?" he whispers.

"Thank goodness." I nod and he passes me to head to the kitchen. I turn to follow. "Where is she?"

Something hits the front door hard, startling me, and I nearly drop the cup and phone.

"Your front porch," Sage says. "You better get to her. Fast."

A finger of dread curls down my spine. I sprint to the entry, shouting, "Logan!" and fling open the door. My breath hitches. "By all that's holy."

Kit's on her knees, one hand gripping the frame to hold herself up. She raises her head, eyes flat, blood trailing from her right ear. "Help," she mutters.

Logan is beside me, and together, we get her to her feet. "What happened?" I ask, guiding her to our sofa.

Her feet stumble over themselves, and she leans heavily on us. "I can't... I don't..."

We ease her onto the cushions and Logan checks her over. "Kit, do you know who I am? Can you understand me?"

She nods, but her head lolls to the side. I grab a dish towel and wipe at the red trailing down her neck. "Did you hit your head?"

"Ava?" She clasps my arm.

"Yes, it's me. Tell me what happened."

"Need...help..."

Logan starts for the kitchen. "I'm calling Doc."

"No," she says. "Just Ava."

Sage sprints in through the still-open door. She joins us, several items in hand. One is a circlet of thin tree branches, forming a crown. Half-inch thorns stick out from it and gray, black, and purple stones have been attached in various spots. She slides it on top of Kit's dark hair. "This will help."

"What is it?" I ask.

"Hawthorn and holly, black tourmaline, labradorite, and amethyst. It will offer her third eye protection and calm her psychic senses."

Kit sighs with relief, her tense body going loose. After a moment, she sits up, blinking. "This is more than tree branches and a few crystals. What else did you add?"

It's the most she's managed to string together since I found her. She seems almost normal. Sage gives a faint self-deprecating smile. "I charmed it with some Archangel Michael mojo."

Logan's eyes hit his hairline.

"How about some water, Kit?" I ask.

"Coffee," she replies, directing the word at Logan. "Black."

He gives me a quizzical look, and at my nod, goes to get it. I sit beside her, wiping the last of the blood off her skin. "Why is your ear bleeding?"

"The pressure." She rubs her temples, a thorn scratching her finger. "Ouch."

"Sorry," Sage adjusts the crown. "The thorns keep negative energy away. Whoever is doing this to you is very powerful."

"Wait, what?"

In the kitchen, I hear Logan talking in a muffled voice.

Sage makes herself comfortable in the recliner, settling her skirt folds around her legs. "A strong psychic is pummeling your third eye with negative energy. I suspect she's trying to overload it. Blow it out."

Kit shakes her head. "The magical grid is clogged and it's building pressure up inside me. I have to clear it out."

Sage leans forward, resting her elbows on her knees.

"There's nothing wrong with the grid, Kit. You're under psychic attack. It's affecting Ava, as well."

"I've also felt that pressure," I tell them both, "right before the world goes gray."

Logan enters and hands Kit a mug. She accepts it and chugs half in a few gulps. "I'm not sure I understand."

"Is there anyone you can think of who dislikes you?" I ask. "Somebody as powerful of a psychic as you are?"

"No, no one," she insists. "I mean, I've known my share of clairvoyants, telepaths, and witches, but I can't think of any who would..." Her voice trails off.

"You *do* know someone," I say.

She downs the rest of the coffee and hands me the cup. "None who could get past my defenses and screw me up like this. Honest."

Logan takes the cup and towel from me. "What about enemies you've made along the way who might hire someone to attack you?"

It's a good question. Kit must think so, too. Her hands flutter around her lap before she rubs the palms on her thighs. "I'm not without enemies, but have you all forgotten that I am, indeed, clairvoyant myself? If anyone were after me, I think I'd know."

"Not if they're warding themselves," Sage says. "And they are. That's the only explanation."

We're all quiet for a moment, and then Kit says, "Well, whoever it is better hope I don't find them because when I do, they're going to get a dose of their own magical medicine."

She starts to rise as if to leave. Logan puts a hand on her shoulder. "Dr. Abernathy is on the way. He'd like to check you over."

"Don't be ridiculous," she blusters. "I don't need a physician."

I grab her hand and tug her next to me. "You were on our doorstep in severe distress only a few moments ago."

"Besides, we have a policy." Logan winks, giving her a cheeky grin. "Anyone who shows up here bleeding has to see the doctor and get the all-clear before we allow them to leave."

Sage comes to her feet. "I'm happy to enforce that policy."

It takes a bit of convincing, but it's three against one, and Kit finally gives in. Mostly, I think, because Logan starts making breakfast and she admits she's famished.

I throw slices of bread in the toaster and set the table while Sage goes to her place to grab her pendulum and map. Her dousing abilities may reveal the culprit's location. This isn't how I anticipated starting the day, but I'm relieved Kit is back.

Sage returns and lays the map of Thornhollow, a purple velvet bag, and her copper pendulum on the table while Logan fries up eggs and bacon. She's brought lemon poppy seed muffins to contribute to the meal and snags coffee before removing them from their paper sack. The toast pops and I butter it as Logan doles out the food on everyone's plates. Once we all have that and drinks, we dive in.

Mama raised me to make polite conversation at the table, steering clear of topics like politics and religion, or anything that riled folks up. "Bad for the digestion," she always claims.

Considering what we're dealing with, talking about a benign subject like the weather seems ridiculous, but anything regarding the festival or tomorrow's ceremony would feel insensitive. I keep quiet, much like the others, and only thank Sage for the muffins, which are delicious, as always.

We've just finished when there's a knock and Doc lets himself in. "Morning," he calls.

"In the kitchen," Logan tells him.

The aging town doctor enters, his black medical bag in hand. He greets each of us and I get him a cup of coffee. There's a muffin left, and he accepts it along with the cup, taking the seat next to Kit that Sage vacates. We clear the table as he looks her over with keen eyes behind his round spectacles. "I hear you're having some nasty migraines."

"I suppose that's one word for it." She pushes back her chair and glances at his bag. "I'm fine now."

His gaze lingers on her hawthorn crown. "Are you in character?" At her frown, he points to the thorny tangle, his voice laced with humor. "Playing Jesus in the parade today?" This earns him a chuckle. He finishes his treat and wipes crumbs from his hands before standing and grabbing his bag.

"I appreciate you making a house call," Kit says.

"Let's have a look at you. Mind removing that?" He points again at her headdress.

"No," Kit and Sage say in unison.

Doc frowns. "Why not?"

"It's protecting me," Kit tells him.

His skeptical look is also curious. "From what, my dear?"

Kit gives me a nervous glance.

I lay a hand on his arm. "You're the expert when it comes to Western medicine and the physical body, but having dated my aunt, you must be familiar with the concept that there are things in this world that you can't detect with your five senses, nor do they line up with traditional logic. We believe we're dealing with something that falls into that rather nebulous category, but still feel it's imperative to have Kit checked for normal causes that you might be better able to detect."

I'm afraid I've been too wordy and vague, but his mouth firms, and then he peers at her. "All right. I'll work around it."

Logan, Sage, and I hang back, making busywork of rinsing the dishes, stacking them in the washer, and cleaning the frying pan, while he examines Kit's ears and shines his penlight into her eyes. She sticks out her tongue as instructed so he can check her mouth and tonsils. He listens to her heart, checks her pulse, and palpates her neck and the parts of her skull he can get to without nicking himself on the thorns. During all this, he asks questions about symptoms, such as dizziness, vomiting, and double vision. She has had all three.

"Okay," he says, packing his instruments away. "I want you to have a CT scan and an MRI. I'll call the hospital and get you an appointment today. If you have any more severe symptoms, you have one of these good folks rush you to the ER, or call 911." He faces us. "She shouldn't be alone until we're sure it's nothing serious."

Logan loops an arm around my shoulders as if he can feel my nervous dread. "We'll make sure somebody's with her at all times."

"I can't afford those tests," Kit says, standing. "I don't have insurance."

Doc gives her a calm smile. "We have a Patient Care Fund. It will cover some of the costs, especially if you're able to volunteer at the clinic."

She narrowed her eyes. "Volunteer to do what? I'm not a nurse."

"There are plenty of things that need attention that have nothing to do with treating patients. You can answer phones, sweep the floors, water the plants. My office is a disaster, and all the windows need washing. I have quite a list, and the more you do, the more your bill will be reduced."

He doesn't wait for her response, and she trails after him. "You want me to wash windows?"

He pauses. "There are a few forms to fill out, and I'll have them ready and waiting. In the meantime, get to the hospital and have that brain checked out."

I hear the door close and she returns to the kitchen, looking shocked. "He thinks I have a tumor, doesn't he? That's why he's ordering the tests."

Sage takes her by the arm and guides her to the chair she'd occupied. "The more we know, the more empowered we are to handle this. Have the tests and, in the meantime, let's see if we can find our psychic assailant. Either way, we'll have all the bases covered."

Appearing somewhat numb, Kit sinks into the seat. Sage spreads out the map and hands the pendulum to her, forcing her fingers to close around it. "Focus," she says. "Put the idea of those tests away for the moment and let the pendulum work. Hold it close to you and let it tap into your aura so I can pick up our invisible psychic."

Kit cups the pendulum to her chest. Sage raises her hands to place them outside of Kit's temples, closing her eyes and whispering. Logan shifts his feet, uncomfortable, but stands with me as we watch.

On occasion, I can see the colors of people's energy fields and, as I open myself up to it, I notice a swirl of bright shades between Sage's palms and Kit's ears. Happy colors, they glow and tumble over each other, growing bigger and seeming to push Sage's hands out farther and farther. I feel myself relax, confident that Kit is going to be okay. I lean into Logan. Between all of us, we will figure this out and make sure my friend is safe and healthy.

Kit smiles. A lovely humming comes from her and the colors grow, undulating with the soft rhythm of her voice.

Sage is not smiling, however. The crease between her brows grows deep. Without warning, Kit stops and her face falls. A thick gray thread of energy wriggles from her ear, the one that was bleeding, and fights against Sage's spell.

Logan's hand tightens on my shoulder. "What's going on?"

He can't see the colors dancing around Kit's head or the gray energy leaking out of her ear. "Looks like we don't need Raven's athame. Our psychic worm has made an appearance."

"I have no clue what that is, but it doesn't sound good."

All at once, Kit cries and drops the pendulum, knocking Sage back as she jumps to her feet. Sage hits the wall and Kit shakes out her hands and reaches for her. "I'm so sorry, Sage. That thing burned me."

She shows us her palms where there are, in fact, red welts.

Sage glances at the map, where the pendulum has fallen. Her face splits with a knowing smile. "Perfect," she says. "You did great."

I grab a fresh dish towel and wrap ice cubes in it to give Kit. "What just happened?"

Sage slides the pendulum aside and taps the map. "We got her. Or him. I couldn't get through the ward to see who it was, but our perpetrator is here in town."

We all move in and stare at the location she's pointing at.

"Carolina Street?" Logan asks. "That's only a few blocks away."

"It can't be." Kit shakes her head adamantly, pressing the cold pack to her burns.

Sage keeps her finger on the spot. "It is."

I know why Kit continues to shake her head. "I'm telling you it's not possible."

"Why not?" Sage demands.

"Because." Kit taps a finger next to hers. "That spot? That's my house."

NINE

The four of us head to Kit's. The one-story ranch she rents is in the center of a block of similar homes, all mid-century builds with minor adornments. Her yard has a single oak, no garage, and the short driveway and narrow sidewalk are lined with gardenia bushes. Their leaves are still green and there's a palm-size milky white bloom scenting the air. We gather on the end of the driveway, her car sitting idle, eyeballing the structure and yard.

I note a faint greenish corona around the house. "Does anything seem out of place to you?"

She shakes her head, drawing a ring with two keys from her pocket as she goes to the side door. It's locked, but Logan insists on entering first, in case our culprit is inside. "Wait here," he tells us.

Anxiety makes my pulse hammer. "Be careful."

My ears sharpen as he disappears, trying to pick up his footsteps. He's quiet as a cat and I worry my fingers, a whisper of cool wind slipping inside my jacket collar. Up and down the street, Kit's neighbors are going about their morning, walking dogs, sending kids to the bus stop, leaving for work. No one even glances our way, yet I feel someone watching. I peer across the street, searching for the source, perhaps encapsulated behind blinds or curtains. "Are you friendly with your neighbors?" I ask Kit quietly.

She follows my gaze. "Don't know most of them beyond saying good morning or waving when we pass in the street. Why?"

Sage looks toward the residence closest to us. "Are there any new to the block?"

Kit shrugs. "These are mostly rentals. Folks move in and out all the time. I haven't noticed anyone unusual, but I'm fairly new to this area myself."

Logan appears. "All clear. I think someone was here, though. Seems like they tossed the place."

Kit brushes past him. "What? You're kidding."

Inside, it does appear ransacked. "Holy goddess," Sage says, giving a soft whistle under her breath. "What were they looking for?"

Kit gives an embarrassed chuckle. "No one broke in." She picks clothes up from the living room floor and tosses them in a chair. Books and papers are strewn about the coffee table among empty cups and dirty plates. She stacks a few and carries them to the small, brightly lit kitchen. More dishes fill the sink. Rows of canned goods and boxes of cereal compete for counter space with a coffee pot and dish drainer. "I'm no housekeeper," she explains, "and the last few weeks have been exceptionally challenging. I didn't have the energy or focus to clean."

I catch a dark shadow moving off the radiator under the window. When I stare straight at it, it's the size and shape of a feline, yet it slips off so quickly, that I can't be sure. "I didn't know you had a cat."

She sets down the plates. "I don't. As you can see, I can barely take care of myself."

Logan and Sage give me questioning looks. Maybe I'm hallucinating again. I shake it off. "Is there a way for us to tell if our psychic was here?" I ask Sage.

She withdraws her pendulum. "Oh, she was here. My tool doesn't lie. What we need to be sure of is that she didn't leave something behind."

"Like what?" Logan asks.

"A hex bag, or some other item she's cursed and planted here to torment Kit. It would certainly be easy to hide in this mess." She murmurs over the pendulum and watches as it begins to move. "I'm going to walk through and see if I can find anything."

I nod and motion at the sink. "While she does that, how about Logan and I help you tidy the place up a bit?"

Kit blushes. "I can't ask you to do that."

Logan shrugs off his jacket and hangs it on the back of a chair. "Nonsense. You've had a rough time. We're happy to help."

He starts on the dishes and I pick through the living room, gathering shoes, throwing newspapers in her recycle bin, and staying out of Sage's way. She works around each space, murmuring and stopping here and there. Kit puts her groceries into the cabinets and starts a load of laundry. Logan takes out the garbage and while he and Kit are busy, I catch Sage and lower my voice. "Any chance you've noticed a ghost cat?"

Her brows dip, the pendulum swinging gently over Kit's nightstand and a collection of items there. "No. Have you?"

"I'm not sure what it was, and I don't usually see animal spirits, but there was something in the kitchen on the radiator. Could I be hallucinating it?"

She peers hard into my eyes and the pendulum stops swinging. I sense her scanning me with her magic. "Was it like before?"

I shake my head. "Not at all. Everything seemed normal except that shadowy blur."

"Hmm." She heads for the kitchen. "Show me where you saw it disappear."

I do. Through the window pane, I hear Logan speaking. There's another male voice, and I figure he's befriended a neighbor and is subtly asking if they've noticed any unusual people in the neighborhood. Sage holds the pendulum over the radiator and it swings wildly, erratically. I point at the place where the shadowy figure disappeared and she guides the pendulum to it. It continues to go crazy. "Why is it acting like that? Is it picking up on the cat?"

"It's picking up on something," she says.

Kit enters, hands full of mail. "On what?"

Her wall phone rings, startling us. She tucks the envelopes under her arm and answers. "Hello?" After confirming her identity, she tosses the mail down and searches for a pen and paper in a drawer. "Yes, okay. Today at one for the CT scan and four for the MRI." She notes the times and locations, the first floor and another in the hospital's west wing. "Got it. Thanks."

She hangs up and stares at her notes. Sage squeezes her hand. "Raven can watch the shop for me. I'll go with you."

"Me, too," I add.

"No, you won't." She tears the paper from its pad and sticks it on her fridge with a magnet. "You both have lives and it's a busy weekend for all of us. I'm perfectly capable of handling this, and we all know my brain is clinically fine. What would help is for you to figure out who's behind the psychic attack and tell me how to stop them."

Sage flicks her gaze at me, back to Kit. "I haven't encountered this sort of thing previously, but it looks like you've picked up a hitchhiker."

Kit leans a hip against the cabinet. "A spirit?"

Sage nods. "Not just any spirit. This isn't your garden variety ghost. I think it may be connected to our spellcaster, but I need to research before I make inaccurate assumptions. For the time being, it's better if you don't stay here."

"You're coming home with us," I insist.

Kit touches her crown. "I have this. I'll be fine."

Logan enters as I loop my arm through hers. "We aren't taking no for an answer." I have the parade at three, but plan to ask Mama to take my place. Kit is my top priority. To him, I say, "Kit has appointments this afternoon at one and four. She's staying with us until then."

"Great." He grabs his jacket. "I'll drive her to the hospital when it's time."

She fusses and argues all the way to the door as we march her out. While the three of them head for the car, I spot a set of glowing green eyes under the radiator as I begin shutting the door. Pressure hits the back of my skull, the world goes monochrome, and my knees buckle.

I hear a hiss that isn't from the heating coils and feel my throat constrict. In the distance, Logan calls my name, but I can't tear my gaze from those malevolent emerald orbs.

My chest tries to pull in air, but all I feel is a burning sensation along my ribs. The world twists in shards of black and white, my lungs heaving, struggling for oxygen. I want to close my eyes, to run, to scream, anything to break this connection.

Persephone appears. "What are you doing on the ground?"

The world tilts and comes back into view in full color. Logan kneels beside me. "Ava! What happened?"

He eases me to my feet and I clutch his arm. The vertigo disappears, and when I peek around Persephone, I see the green eyes have as well. "I'm okay."

Sage and Kit join us. "Are you sure?" Sage asks.

My head bobs a yes, even as my brain screams *no*. "I just need to go home."

None of them buy it, but I insist, and Logan helps me to the car. Sage lingers a moment, peering into the kitchen before locking the door. Persephone hovers on the drive as we back out.

You and I will discuss this at home, I mentally tell her.

She frowns and blinks out of sight.

TEN

On the way, I text Brax to tell him Kit is back and having tests that afternoon. I ignore Logan's looks of concern, smiling as if nothing happened. Rosie is arriving when we pull up, and after everyone exchanges good mornings, Sage hoofs it across the street to open her shop.

Logan doesn't want to leave me, and we have a discussion about my blood sugar, eating enough, and alleviating my stress. Through it all, I act normal, retrieving my cup of coffee, accepting the granola bar he hands me, and then chatting with Rosie about the day's schedule. Reluctantly, he takes Moxley for his daily walk.

Rosie and I review the items on my list while Kit ambles through the house, asking what she can do. Rosie questions her crown and Kit bluntly supplies the basics.

Rosie rubs the cross that's always hung at her neck but doesn't say much beyond she hopes we work it out.

Kit can't sit still, so I have her call the florist to confirm that the bulk of the flowers for Saturday will be delivered by five. Betty assures her they will.

Rhys shows up shortly after that and he and Kit huddle in the kitchen, Kit recapping once again what happened to her and that Sage is formulating a plan. Rhys begs her to consider doing readings that evening at The Toad and she agrees.

I think it's a bad idea, but it's none of my business. After he leaves, telling me he'll see me at the parade, Kit wags a finger at me. "I know you don't approve of me working tonight, but I'm a private investigator, as well as a psychic. It's time for me to do my job. If another psychic is after me, what better way for me to get a lead than at The Toad? They may have been right under my nose this whole time. If they're watching and keeping tabs on me, they'll be hanging around there."

She has a point.

"Jenn's running late," Rosie calls to me. "Yaz is sick."

I stop at her desk on the way to mine. "Anything serious?"

Rosie shakes her head. "She ate some dirt and upchucked. Doc says she's fine, just being a normal kid, but may be off her food for a day or so. Jenn said to tell you she's really sorry and will get here as soon as she can."

Since she was handling the garden for the staged photos, I debate waiting for her to show or doing it myself. I hurry to my office and grab my purse, fumbling inside for my keys. "Looks like I better squeeze in a trip to the vineyard."

"I can go with you," Kit says. "Help out."

Never look a psychic gift horse in the mouth. I can decorate and keep an eye on her. "I'll take you up on that. Maybe you can assist with a ghost problem, too."

Instead of heading to the car, I lead her out to the gazebo. She stands next to me at the base of the steps. "This is where you saw the pregnant gal?"

"Yes. I want to get her name." She wasn't hanging around at the moment, but I'm sure she was no hallucination. "Any chance you can reach out and, I don't know, touch the wood or something and get a hit? Learn who she is and how she died?"

Closing her eyes, she drags in a deep breath, exhaling slowly as she grips the railing. Her eyes move under her lids and I feel a pressure building behind mine. I blink a couple of times but the pressure grows, along with the sense someone is approaching.

Tabitha makes her way to us, curiosity on her youthful face. "Is the hawthorn helping?"

I nod. An icy chill slides over my arms, down my legs. Glancing at Kit, I see sweat beading on her forehead. Her hand clenches the railing, her knuckles white. "Kit? Are you getting anything?" I don't want to break her concentration but I'm concerned about her wellbeing.

She responds through gritted teeth. "Something is keeping me from accessing her."

"Let me aid ye." My grandmother takes her other hand.

Kit's head snaps back, but her grasp on the railing loosens. The ghost pops into view.

"Did you tell her?" she asks me.

"Is your name Maria Grace? Your mother is Nettie?"

She acknowledges both with a dip of her chin. "I can't go back. I don't know the way home."

"I can help with that. First, I need to know how you died. Did Bobby kill you?"

Her gaze goes beyond me, searching the yard. "Is he

here?" She floats around the interior of the gazebo, calling for him. "Bobby? Where are you? I knew you'd come for us."

The pressure fills my head and I sway, clutching the stair rail to keep from falling. The instant I touch it, the world turns silvery and frost coats the air. Maria Grace cries out and I pivot to follow where her attention has landed behind me. A fleeting spirit sails down the hill and vanishes at the creek. She sobs, her hand rubbing her belly, then turns on me, seething. "You tricked me!"

And then my grandmother is next to me. Warmth floods my body and the world returns to normal. The ghost disappears and I find myself staring at a frowning Kit. She grips my other hand, the three of us forming a triangle. "I saw it. *Her*," she says. "All of it." She rubs my chilled fingers between hers. "It was weird, but kind of cool. As if I was looking through your eyes. Now I know what you meant about the world turning monochrome."

"Time riding," Tabitha says with a note of awe in her voice.

"What?" I ask.

"Fragments of in-between time. Ye be slipping into and between them, riding them."

Kit's brow furrows more deeply. "When I peeked at you, you were...transparent." She clears her throat. "Like a ghost."

"Ye be here and there," Tabitha says, nodding.

My brain doesn't compute. "I turn into a ghost?"

Tabitha shakes her head. "Your physical body appears less corporeal because your spirit is over there."

"Where is *there*?"

"One foot is in this world of the living." She squints up at the sky. "The other be in the world of death." Her eyes return to mine. "Some earthbound are stuck in the in-between, a place without time, as we know it. When this happens, ye be slipping into that plane to talk to them, rather than pulling them into ours. Takes a mighty power to meet them there. Few can go visit and not..."

She trails off, biting her bottom lip, but I get the gist. "Die," I finish.

"Which ye have already done more than once." She looks pensive. "Mayhap that be why ye can do it. Your spirit has moved through timeless spaces. It's changed something inside ye. It allows ye to access the fragments the ghosts are caught in."

"Is that what happened at my house?" Kit asks. "When you staggered and fell? I thought you saw something and then you seemed, I don't know, gray. Pale. Less there."

I rub my head. A timpani drum has begun to beat inside. "Why now?"

"Because of me," Kit says with utter surety. "There is for certain a magical nexus here, and I've been pouring so much into it to clear the imaginary blockage, I've opened up more of your abilities."

All I care about is preventing further excursions into that gray, lifeless world. "How do I stop it?"

We look at Tabitha. She chews her lip again in contemplation. "I'm not sure ye can. Not completely." At my expression of frustration, she backpedals. "I'm certain we can limit it. Let me think on it and talk to Sage. It's not a skill of mine, but I shall figure it out. Meanwhile, speak to your friend, Winter. Ask if she's experienced such things and if she and her sisters have any ideas on controlling it."

Yes, Winter. She's a highly skilled medium with far more

experience than me. "I'll do that." The throbbing over my brows eases. "Please don't say anything to Logan. I don't want him worried about me."

"Too late," Kit says. "I thought he might cart you off to the clinic, he was so concerned when you nearly fainted at my house."

As Tabitha leaves and I make a mental note to call Winter, Kit and I return inside. Filling a travel mug with coffee, I tell her what Nettie said the previous day, as well as what I witnessed in the barn with the gangsters. We head out, discussing ideas on how to help all of the phantoms.

Logan arrives from the dog walk as we're climbing into my car. "Jenn can't set up the picture station, so I have to do it," I tell him. "Kit's going with me and I'll take her to her first appointment from there."

Moxley is panting and Logan checks his watch. "I'll shift my ten o'clock with the dean and come with you. You've got enough to handle without taking over for Jenn."

"That's why Kit's going. Don't reschedule. If you finish before noon, call and check on our progress. If we're not done, you can finish it up while we're at the hospital."

"You're sure?" At my nod, he kisses me goodbye. "All right. I'll see you later, but if you so much as sneeze, I want you to call me."

I love this man and tell him so before I return his kiss. Watching him and the dog go inside, I catch myself smiling like a schoolgirl.

Kit sighs. "I wish I had that." I lift a brow and she laughs. "Not him. The love you two share."

I toss the keys across the hood to her. While I'd like to dig deeper into her affair with Howard, I force myself not to say a word. "You're driving. I need to practice my speech and you're my victim."

"Great," she says, with a total lack of enthusiasm. "Maybe I should take my chances with my attacker."

"About that." I buckle up as she starts the car. "There's something you need to know."

ELEVEN

"A shadow cat? In my house?" Kit mutters something unintelligible but it has an edge to it like a curse. We're on Main Street, and she whips the car left to do a U-turn in the middle of the intersection. Both sides are decorated for the parade. Bright orange traffic blockades are lined up in the courthouse parking lot, waiting to be stationed at the entrances a few hours from now in order to divert vehicles from the route the floats and marching band will take. "How do we get it out?"

I grip the dash, my body going sideways. Sage wanted me to wait to tell Kit for this very reason. "Sage is working on that. We don't know exactly what it is, or why it's there, and you have to stay away until we do. I know it's upsetting, but I thought you should know."

She accelerates. Her crown tips. "Why did you wait until now to tell me?"

Thankful for my seatbelt, I infuse my voice with calm. "Because, if I can now visit this in-between plane, and I can figure out how to do it safely, I think I can use the shadow cat to track our culprit. It all makes more sense now. Except," I put a hand on her shoulder, "I need you to trust me and wait until after the ceremony for me to experiment with it. That means, no going back to your place. If you need something, one of us will get it. You're staying with Logan and me until we figure it out."

She sets her jaw, but after another block, she pulls over. Staring straight ahead, she remains quiet. I do, too, realizing we were only a few houses from her rental, the October sun seeming softer here, and only a couple of thin clouds in the sky.

I see the moment she gives in. Her shoulders slump. "Fine, but just until Sunday. I'll help you get ready for the ceremony, and afterward, we'll tackle my issue."

I remove my hand from her shoulder and straighten her crown. "Thank you. I know how hard it is to stand down and wait. If I knew exactly what to do right now, I'd be more than happy to do it."

"I know you would."

She's about to put the shifter back in gear and turn us around when a Jaguar passes by. It doesn't register with me at first, but I see her eyes narrow as she tracks it. "What is *he* doing here?"

I sit forward. The car is a forest green and there's a college parking sticker on the windshield. "Is that who I think it is?"

She pulls away from the curb. "Oh, yeah. That's him. I'd know that vehicle anywhere."

"Maybe he's lost. He's not familiar with our town, is he?"

It cruises past her place, slowing. "Or maybe he's looking for me."

"What do you want to do? You can't take him inside, even if he does want to talk to you."

But the dean keeps going, accelerating and turning at the end of the block. "Guess it's a moot point," she says. Her voice holds a tinge of sadness.

"We can go after him. Invite him to my house. You can see what he wants."

Her head shake is adamant, dislodging the hawthorn once more. She shoves at it with one hand and wheels into her driveway with the other. Turning around, she steers us toward the main road. "I have nothing to say to him."

I don't believe that, but I let it drop. "What do you think about my pregnant ghost? Did Bobby kill her?"

"If he did, and that's why she's stuck here, she'd want revenge, right? She doesn't seem to want anything more than for him to come and get her so she can go home to her mother."

I consider the other man I saw in the barn who had watched me, silent and oozing malcontent. "Maybe Bobby didn't. Either way, I'm betting he's one of the ghosts in the barn. He and the other fellow hanging out with him need to move on before my reception."

On the highway heading north, we pass a tractor with a wagon of hay bales. "I see you found your phone."

"Sherlock discovered a ghost stole it. It's the girl's mother, Nettie. Apparently, she's a kleptomaniac."

Kit snorts. "That's a new one. She must be strong. Are you going to cross her as well?"

I typically cajole any and all of the earthbound to move on. Those who linger here became vicious and predatory. "In the best interest of everyone, I need to. They should be reunited with family, be reincarnated, if that's their lot in life."

"So you believe in that stuff?"

"Reincarnation? You bet I do. Don't you?"

"Some days I wish I didn't." At the questioning glance I shoot across to her, she zeros in on the road more intently. "I hear karma is a nasty—"

Before she can finish, Persephone pops into the backseat. "It is, but yours is good. Don't worry about coming back as a rat or skunk."

Kit nearly drives off the road. I yank the steering wheel to keep us from jetting into the ditch. Gravel kicks up from the tires, peppering the underside of the car, and the rear fishtails. "Don't do that," I growl at my guardian angel. Then I turn to my friend, who is breathing heavily and white-knuckling the wheel. Twice in one day, I've made that happen. She may never talk to me again. "You can see her?"

Kit's eyes dart to the rearview, then once more to the road. "No, but I hear her."

Persephone can show herself to anyone she chooses. "Let Kit see you," I order. I know how uncomfortable disembodied voices can be. "And next time give us some warning, would you?"

Persephone laughs, as if this is all lighthearted fun. She must become visible because I notice Kit glance at the mirror and stiffen as Persephone leans forward and pats her shoulder. "As I said, your karma is a-okay."

Kit gives a tremulous smile. "You sure know how to make an entrance, don't you?"

Another laugh fills the interior as we approach the welcome sign to the vineyard. "It's one of my specialties." She winks at Kit. "I've got tons more."

As Kit turns up the driveway, she catches my eye. "I just bet you do."

"I hope you're here to help," I tell Persephone. "There are at least three spirits I need cleared from this property before Saturday."

I hear the jingle of her bracelets. "So make the lighted door and get them through it. You don't need me for that."

"It's not that easy, I'm afraid." One of the family's large dogs barks and runs alongside the car as we arrive at the parking area. I haven't seen him in ages. Kit stops and I unfasten my seatbelt, turning to pin Persephone with a glare. "Kit and I are setting up the garden for the staged photos. While we do that, you're going to visit Nettie and get more info on her daughter and who the two cognizant male ghosts in the barn are."

"You know I can't do that."

"You can and you will. Or should I say, you'll figure out a loophole in your spirit guide regulations that gets me the info."

Her lips drag down and she appears confused. "There are no loopholes."

"Sherlock?" I call.

On cue, he appears next to her. "You rang?"

Persephone starts to argue, flustered. I grin and hold up my hand. "We all have our assignments. Let's get to it."

TWELVE

The butler, Winston, informs me Helen has gone to town to get her hair done. That explains the dogs running loose—he has a sweet spot for them.

To be honest, I'm relieved she's not here. On the front veranda, I motion toward the top of the hill that looks out over the rolling fields of dormant grapevines. The terrace and garden pavilion there have been designated for the photo shoot. Helen insisted on an engagement announcement for the Thornhollow newspaper a few months back, when the valley was lush and green, right before the harvest started. I have to admit those pictures turned out beautifully, and while the landscape in the valley is nowhere as pretty this time of year, it remains an impressive backdrop. "Kit and I will be decorating up there," I tell him.

"Of course." He gives a nod. "May I be of service?"

"Do you have time?"

"My jobs today are finished and my duties are suspended until Mrs. Cross returns." He steps out and closes the door. "Besides, I could use some fresh air. Do you mind the dogs?"

I've always liked him; now even more so. "Not at all."

Together, we stroll across the lawn and climb the stone steps embedded in the hill to join Kit at the arbor entrance to the garden. The vineyard typically sees plenty of tourists this time of year, but due to the reception, that's been stifled, since we couldn't have an endless stream of visitors coming and going while preparing. Not only are Logan's parents laying out a ton of money for this, they're losing income due to it.

I introduce Kit to Winston and examine the area while he pulls work gloves from a nearby covered bench. He's not the main gardener, but I've seen him futzing with planters around the place before. "On Saturday, Betty will add fresh floral arrangements to the trellis and freshen the jardinières." I've always called them urns, but Helen informed me she prefers the French term.

The giant concrete planters weep ivy trails and massive ferns grow from their centers, still green, thanks to the mild fall. Most of the garden's perennials have faded but a few gardenias are blooming, scenting the air with a light fragrance. I pause a minute to draw it in, forgetting briefly about ghosts, psychic attacks, and time slips.

"What would you like us to do?" Winston asks.

"We need to wind solar lights through the trellises and arbor, and move that obelisk"—I point to the nearest one that rises as tall as my shoulder—"behind the gazing ball."

The three of us get to it, me giving instructions and stepping back on occasion to get a broader perspective. Once half the lights are strung, I flinch. "We need to test those."

Jenn always does this before leaving The Wedding

Chapel, and again once she's at the location, carrying replacement bulbs. I'm distracted and forgot to be sure they would work until now.

Winston does the honors, and I'm relieved when they light up like it's Christmas.

At one point, as I'm pretending to be the photographer and lining up a shot, movement in the distance catches my eye. I face the farmhouse and see a curtain flutter in an upstairs window. At first, I assume it's Helen's maid, but the hair on the back of my neck rises and I realize it's a ghost. Not Sherlock or my guardian angel. Nettie.

Returning to the arbor, I fiddle with a smaller planter. "Do you know anything about a maid named Nettie who worked here in the late 1920s?" I ask Winston.

He brushes his gloved hands together. "Does this have anything to do with you being in her room yesterday?"

"You do know about her."

He smiles, his gentle voice carrying a hint of amusement. "She had a reputation when she worked here. Mrs. Cross often uses her, and what happened to her, as a horror story with the new help. Scares them straight, I guess."

"Is that so? What happened?"

"During The Great Depression, the folks that lived here barely held onto the place. They farmed, raised animals, and sold off most of their belongings. Nettie worked for them during Prohibition. She didn't approve of the still that produced whiskey, but she needed her job, so kept her mouth shut. When times got tough, the whiskey sales kept the bank from taking the land and house. However, Nettie's daughter had fallen in with a bootlegger."

"Bobby V," I state.

He nods. "His boss, a man named Raymond Grimes,

from across the county line didn't like the competition the Cross family gave him. He pressured Bobby and Maria Grace, Nettie's daughter, to help him steal the whole distillery. No one outside the immediate family knew where it was hidden, but Nettie had found out. Her daughter went to her and told her Grimes was going to kill Bobby if he didn't destroy it, and since Nettie hated alcohol and its consumption, she told them where it was hidden, believing it was God's will. Turned out that Bobby and Raymond simply dismantled the whole thing and took it across the county line so Grimes could use it himself. It destroyed the one solid line of income the family had, but they couldn't go to the police, since it was illegal."

Kit straightens from picking dead leaves off the ivy around the white trellis. "What did they do?"

"Nettie wasn't repentant and her employer turned her out. But she discovered she'd been had and was so angry at Bobby V and Grimes, she decided to get even. She convinced her daughter to spy on them and learn the location of Grimes' main still. The girl, who was pregnant, vanished shortly after that. Nettie swore revenge on Bobby V, claiming he killed her, but everyone knew Raymond Grimes was most likely the reason for the girl's disappearance. Nettie was destitute and begged the family to take her back, and they did, but she'd lost it over her missing daughter. They found her dead in her room shortly after prohibition ended. Said she'd poisoned herself out of grief and guilt. A lot of folks thought the family might have done it, or maybe Grimes got to her. No one knows for sure."

"Did they ever find Maria Grace's body?" I ask casually.

"Not to my knowledge. Bobby claimed he sent her away, fearing Grimes might kill her because of her mama, and the fact they both knew too much about his operation, but when he went looking for her after Grimes was killed, he couldn't find her."

"What a mess," Kit says, and I nod my agreement.

We finish and Winston offers us a drink. I get a call from Logan, and tell Kit to go on to the house. I answer my phone. "Hey, there. How'd the meeting go?"

"Interesting," he says. "I'm free now. I can help."

I check the time—it's nearing noon. "Winston pitched in and we're done. How about you meet me at the diner for a quick lunch? Kit's not supposed to eat before her test, but I'm starving. Can you call Queenie and order two specials so they're ready when we get there? Then we can take Kit to her appointment."

"You know me, I don't turn down food."

"I want to hear about your meeting with the dean, but not while she's with us, okay?"

"Roger that." He grunts. "I don't know the man well but he likes things straightforward and he's all about reason and intellect. Logic, facts, science. You get the picture. He questioned me about our friendship with her. Said we should reconsider how much we trust her."

My hackles rise. "That's out of line. He has no say in who we befriend or—"

"I know," he interrupts. "Which is why there isn't much else to tell about the meeting. I turned down the job offer."

My ruffled feathers relax. "You're my hero, you know that?"

"I don't think I've heard the last from him, though. He backtracked pretty quickly and apologized. He's desperate for me to fill in for Abbey. Honestly, I think he's still carrying a torch for Kit and his bluster about her is more for show than anything because of Drew."

While I can't see Nettie, I feel her gaze prickling against my skin. I walk toward the veranda, wondering if Sherlock had any luck with her. "Drew came with him?"

"Yeah, it was odd. He sat in on our meeting. Didn't say much, but he seemed tense, keyed up."

As I arrive at the double doors, Kit walks out and hands me a glass of tea, Winston following. The dogs lie on the wood planks, wagging lazily. "I'm sorry it didn't go better. So Kit and I will meet you at The Bee Hive in ten?"

"I'll get us a table and order the food."

We say our goodbyes and disconnect. I sip my tea, wishing I had time to hunt down Nettie and cross her over, but I'm ready for a break from ghosts. "Lunch is on me," I tell Winston, "if you want to come with us to The Bee Hive."

He shoots a glance at Kit but shakes his head. "I appreciate the offer, but I better get back to work." His eyes slide to her again as he adds, "Raincheck?"

She smiles and finishes off her drink, handing the glass to him. "Thanks for your help and for not making fun of the reason for my headgear."

Did she tell him? I'm shocked, but the grin he gives her could light up the entire town. "I'd like to schedule a reading when you're back to work."

"You got it," she says. "I'd fit you in tonight, but I'm over-booked as it is. Maybe next week?"

"Text me."

In the car, she's still smiling. "That went well," I say.

She maneuvers the car down the drive. "This place looks like the queen of England is attending your wedding. But it is beautiful."

I chuckle. "That's not what I meant. Someone has a new admirer."

She opens her mouth, shuts it. Sends a glance out the window. "He's nice."

"That's it?"

"Are you going to practice that speech on me or not? And by the way, don't think I'm not eating lunch."

I fear the happiness on her face is going to be replaced if I do recite my speech, but arguing with her over whether she can eat or not is perilous. "Doctors orders—"

"They're checking my brain, not my gut, so save it."

Okay, then. I pull out my notes. "You're sure you want to hear this?"

We hit the road into town. "If it will keep you off my back about lunch and cute admirers, go for it."

So I do.

THIRTEEN

The Bee Hive is bursting at the seams when we arrive. During the summer, Queenie and Brax took the narrow alley between The Hive and his coffee bar and created an outdoor seating area. One of those tables is reserved for us and as we weave through the crowd that spills onto the sidewalk, a server waves us toward it. "Jackie will be out with your drinks momentarily."

An umbrella shades us from the sun and I remove my sweater. It's a tad dirty from our work. Logan is already there, talking to a couple at another table, and waves. He begs off from them and joins us. "I'm starving."

"Me, too," Kit agrees. "I haven't been able to eat for days because of my..." She glances around. The seating is tight and we can hear many of their conversations. "Problem," she finishes, placing her napkin in her lap.

"I thought you weren't supposed to for two hours beforehand," Logan says.

"Save your breath," I tell him before she can start in. "Kit does things her way." She's garnered a few looks from the other guests because of her headpiece, but most are preoccupied with the delicious food and their companions. "While you're having the scan," I inform her, "I'll call Sage and see if she's come up with ideas for us."

Jackie arrives with our beverages. She's harried, plopping the glasses down and wiping her hands on her apron. "Your meals will be out shortly, and congrats on your nuptials."

"We're going to need a third special," Kit says. "And I'll take the bill."

Logan shakes his head. "Lunch is on me."

Jackie shrugs and hustles away, clearing a table where the guests just left.

While we wait, I gloat a bit to Logan, explaining that Kit awarded me a gold star for my speech. "You and Mama should get the credit," I admit, "but my delivery makes the words come alive."

He gives me a bemused smile. "Is that so?"

I nod. "Kit said so."

She raises her hands in surrender to Logan's quizzical brow lift. "She has Dixie's flair for inspiring folks. After hearing it, I was bubbling with enthusiasm and ready to visit all the downtown stores and book a weekend retreat at the B&B. And I live here."

We share a chuckle. "Bubbling with enthusiasm?" I make a face. "I don't think I've ever seen you bubble."

"It's exceptionally rare. I guess after the nightmare I've been living for the past few weeks, I feel like I have a new lease on life. I sure hope I don't have to walk around with a wreath on my head for the rest of it."

A man and woman take the vacant table and call greetings to us. I can't remember their names, but Logan does, addressing them. "Clarice, Harris. Beautiful day, isn't it? Perfect kick-off for the festival."

"I sure hope it stays nice for your big occasion," Clarice says. Her toothy smile doesn't reach her eyes. "I heard it's supposed to storm." She glances at me, her eyes filled with jealousy. Her aura flares a sickly green. "Guess not even the mayor, nor the great Helen Cross, can control Acts of God."

"Rain isn't an Act of God," Kit says, sipping her tea. "That's Mother Nature." Clarice blinks, speechless. "Technically, an Act of God refers to a disaster, like an earthquake or a hurricane."

Another blink. "What...?"

Harris chuckles. "Y'all know what she means."

Logan squeezes my arm when I open my mouth to retort. I close it and strain to stop my eye roll. There are always plenty of people eager to stir up drama here, as if wishing ill on others might relieve their own misery. Add in those who are jealous of the fact my business is successful and that I'm marrying one of the famous Cross brothers, and you've got somebody who trips all my triggers.

"It's not going to storm," Kit says.

All glances land on her and she gives a wicked smile.

"How do you know?" Clarice asks, wrinkling her pert nose.

Kit taps her temple. "I know everything. Like how you embarrass your poor husband every time you go out in public, and the fact you run up the credit card bills so high, he can work a month of Sundays and never pay them off."

Gasps erupt around us and I realize the other customers have fallen quiet.

"Well, I never!" The woman stands abruptly, knocking her chair back, her husband gawking at Kit.

"How did you know?" he echoes.

His wife smacks him on the shoulder. "I'm making a complaint to the owner."

At that moment, Queenie appears, a paper bag in hand. "Here's your meals." Talk about psychic. She hands it to Harris, who's on his feet now. "On the house. You should go." She gives Clarice a pointed look that could melt plastic. "FYI, I don't tolerate troublemakers. You want to come back, you check your attitude at the curb, you hear?"

Clarice raises her voice and argues, but her husband, flushed with embarrassment, drags her away, mumbling apologies to all of us. His wife flings one last statement over her shoulder at us. "You can forget our wedding gift, Logan! We won't be attending."

I can't help myself. Helen has a lot of friends and frenemies that she's invited to the reception, many of whom I don't know or particularly like. "We have a waiting list. I'm sure the Robinsons will be thrilled to fill your spots. You won't be missed."

It's a good thing Harris and Queenie are between us.

As the two of them push the raging Clarice to the parking lot, Kit giggles. "There's that flair for inspiring folks."

Logan shakes his head as he rises. "Maybe we should take our lunch to go, too."

Queenie returns, overhearing him. "Splendid idea. Meet me up front."

Soon we're home, and Jenn arrives to take over the phones from Rosie, assuring us that Yaz is fine. Rosie leaves and Kit, Logan, and I gather in the kitchen, hurriedly scarfing down our food. I should be contrite about my outburst—St. Helen will blow a gasket—but I'm not. I bring

Logan up to speed on the current ghost situation and what Winston told us concerning Nettie.

"You saw her daughter this morning? In our backyard? Why didn't you tell me?"

I wish I had a better answer, but I give the only one I can. "It's been a bizarre day, even by my standards."

Little did I know how outlandish it was about to get.

FOURTEEN

Sage storms into the house, looking bedraggled. "I don't have much time," she says, combing strands of hair back from her face. They've come loose from her braid. "Raven is watching the shop for me, but we're swamped."

Since we only have ten minutes before we have to leave for the hospital, I simply nod. "Understood. What did you find?"

She sinks into the chair next to Kit. "Did you tell them about what you saw at Kit's?"

"I did. They know everything I know."

"Great. The shadow cat is a spirit familiar. You know about witches and their familiars, right?"

Kit shifts in her chair. "They help witches with their magic."

Sage gives a nod and continues. "They act as amplifiers, similar to batteries, when a witch needs more magic than he or she can handle during a spell casting, to ramp up their power. In this case, the familiar is a ghost. It probably was the witch's in life, and now continues to help her in spirit."

"She killed her cat in order to do this?" Kit asks. "That's terrible."

Sage looks grim but rushes to reassure her. "A sane witch would never do that under any circumstances." I can see that she wants to believe this but may have some doubts. "My guess is it died of natural causes, and she decided not to let it go. As we all know, it's hard to say goodbye to our pets when they die, especially for a witch who uses theirs as part of his or her magic. It's a deeper connection than pretty much anything you can imagine. Like a child you've given birth to and raised."

"But how can a ghost cat amplify her power?" Logan asks, tossing down his napkin. "Doesn't it need a physical body to contain the magic?"

Sage's eyes take on a new light. "That's what I thought, too. I've never actually run into anyone who used a spirit in this way. The physical body of a familiar is a container, but without that, the witch has to spell the spirit in order to create a border of magic around it, like us casting one to protect your property. It's not so much a container as a moving perimeter. Does that make sense?"

Kit waves a hand through the air. "Whatever. How do we get rid of it? Can Ava simply cross it to the afterlife? I want it out of my house. Now."

"Spirit animals are out of my wheelhouse," I say. "I've only ever helped people over."

Sage sits back with an exhausted sigh. "Animals *are* differ-ent. I believe they have souls, and go back to the Creator, but you can't reason with their spirits like you can a human's. You can't trick or manipulate them to move on. This is particularly challenging since it's tied to the witch in more ways than one. The spell that creates the cat's ability to continue to hold her magic and amplify her power also creates a stronger connection to this physical plane. We have to release the familiar from the witch's control before it can move on. I suspect, that if we can lift the spell, the spirit will naturally leave. However, the ghost cat is our best means of tracing the magic back to the source—its owner. Only then, can we eliminate the witch."

Kit's mouth drops open. "You want me to let that thing stay in my house?"

"Just until I can figure out how to trace the magic to its origin."

I swallow the last bite of my sandwich. "Do you know how to do that?"

"Not yet," she admits. "But Raven and I have resources. After we finish today, we're going to visit the magical library."

The sisters own a metaphysical store eight miles away called Chicks with Gifts Emporium. Raven has taken over since Sage opened her tea shop here. Next door is a public library that covers for the Magical Library of Witches and Wizards. "It's filled with the history of witches and wizards in this area," I explain to Kit.

"Not only histories," Sage tells her, "but also grimoires and all types of mystical handbooks. I'm sure we'll find what we need in those."

Kit appears both intrigued and wary. "Do you want help? I'll need some parameters since I don't know what I'm looking for, but I'll do whatever I can."

I slide my chair back and stand. "We can help, too. Right

now, we need to get Kit to the hospital for her first appointment."

"I don't need tests," Kit says. "We know what's wrong with me. How am I going to get through them without losing my mind, anyway? I have to take this off, don't I?" She points to her crown.

"That's right. No jewelry or metal, either," Sage tells her. She pulls a marker from her skirt pocket. "A tattoo, however, is allowed."

"You're going to tattoo me?"

"Raven suggested it. I don't know why I didn't think of it earlier. I can put sigils on your body to ward you. Since they are temporary, it will only work for short bursts, then need to be refreshed, but it should do the trick for the afternoon."

Kit looks skeptical. "I still think I should forget about going. It's a waste of time, and you all have important things to do."

Logan clears the table of our dishes, setting the plates in the sink before he fishes out his car keys. "Remember our policy."

Sage wiggles her fingers at Kit. "I can't do any research yet, anyway. Too many customers." When Kit reluctantly gives in, Sage draws a mark on the inside of Kit's left wrist. She puts a second on the back of her neck. "Good. Now go and we'll meet up after closing time."

"Deal." Kit gestures for us to follow her and we form a conga line leaving the kitchen. "See you then."

Due to traffic pouring into town for the parade, we are five minutes late, but as per normal, the hospital is running behind. There are fewer people here, but plenty of ghosts. I ignore them as Logan and I stay in the waiting room while

Kit disappears behind a solid door with the nurse who calls her name. We are alone, and I pull out my speech.

"Nervous?" Logan asks.

"I don't want to disappoint anyone, especially Mama."

He kicks an ankle up on the opposite knee. "You won't. Regardless of how she acts, she's as proud as any mother could be of you."

It's reassuring to hear that, although I still have that place inside of me that feels like I'm a disappointment to her. She's an incredible woman and hard to live up to. "Your mother is especially proud of you, too," I tell him. "She plans for you to take over the winery. Did you know?"

He draws back and frowns. "She said that?"

I nod and relate what she told me.

"Hunh. She used to talk about Chuck and I co-owning and operating it together. That was her dream. She knows he's the obvious choice—I have no interest in running it, and he loves it. He's got the experience, and he's who she goes to when she has issues. He's great at troubleshooting."

"I'm only repeating what she said." I read through my speech, silence falling. The speaker comes on, a doctor being paged. We hear squeaky wheels and the sound of rubber soles in the hall. Behind the desk, the department receptionist is on a call, setting up an appointment. "If the dean hadn't been such a jerk, would you have taken the temporary teaching position?"

The question pulls him from his inner reverie. "Probably. I sort of like teaching."

His passing it up because of my friend doesn't sit well with me. Howard was rude, but at least I wouldn't have to be around him. Logan wouldn't much either, and the students would learn a ton from him. "Maybe you should consider taking it."

"What?" He shakes his head. "No way. Not if Howard is going to besmirch Kit."

I can't help the smile that spreads across my face. "You're pretty cool, Attorney Cross, or should I call you Dauntless?"

He grins. "Still glad you're marrying me?"

"Since we already tied the knot in June, I don't have much choice, do I?"

He pinches my side, making me laugh. The receptionist glances up. Logan waits until she's distracted again and lowers his voice. "Is it bad in here? With the ghosts, I mean."

Places like this are full of them, which is why I typically stay away. Currently, an older woman is watching us from behind the desk with rheumy eyes. I don't think she's stuck here, but rather is connected to the receptionist. She confirms this when she says, "Tell her I heard her when she was at my deathbed. I know what she said, and yes, I forgive her. I hope she forgives me, too." She tells me they fought, and what about.

I sigh and cock my chin in that direction. "I need to deliver a message," I say. Logan is used to this. As the receptionist hangs up, I ask the ghost, "What's your name?"

"Eleanor," she replies. "My grandkids called me Bunny." She smiles and explains why.

I pocket my speech, take a fortifying breath, and approach the desk. "Hi," I say when the receptionist glances up. Her name tag reads Olivia. "I'm Ava, and I know this sounds odd, but your grandmother, Bunny, wants you to know she heard what you said at her bedside before she transitioned." It's a term I prefer over 'died' these days. There is an afterlife and no one truly ceases to exist, we simply shift into another version of ourselves. A *better* version. "She wants you to know she forgives you for the things you said about Cliff, and she hopes you forgive her, too."

Olivia blinks, sputters, and jerks her gaze around as if her grandmother might materialize in front of her. "How do you know any of that?"

"I'm a medium." It's taken a year for me to be able to admit it without stumbling over the word or cringing when I confess it. "Spirits speak to me."

Her eyes narrow. "Sure they do. Have you seen a therapist about these delusions?"

If only that were the cure.

Bunny chuckles. "She gets her skepticism from me. Her tenacity, too."

"You're going to have to give me something specific that only you and Olivia know," I tell the ghost.

Olivia gawks at me. "What?"

"She always liked catching fireflies in my backyard," Bunny says with a smile of remembrance. "She named one Swan when she was seven. It clung to her for an hour, that little light barely a glimmer. Eventually, it flew off, but she'd already named it. Made me promise not to tell her brothers. They would have made fun of her."

I repeat the story, watching Olivia's expression turn into a mix of shock and struggle, then belief. "You couldn't know that." It comes out in a tremulous whisper. Her eyes dart about. "Bunny?"

The discussion between the three of us continues for another minute and Olivia begins crying. The solid door to the side opens and Kit emerges. "Bunny has to go now," I tell Olivia. I envision the doorway of white light. "And so do I."

Bunny stares at it with a look of bliss. "Tell her I love her and will always be with her."

I repeat her message, and then we leave a crying, but seemingly happy Olivia to her thoughts.

In the elevator, I question Kit. "How did it go?"

She toys with the crown, which she's kept with her. "Fine, I guess. The sigil seems to work, but I couldn't tell from the reactions of the operator or nurse if they saw anything unusual." The elevator dings and we pick up more passengers, both living and dead. It suspends our conversation until we're on the main floor. We have plenty of time to get back to Thornhollow before the parade kickoff. I want to practice in front of my full-length mirror and maybe even try on my dress.

"Did you do your ghost-whispering thing back there?" Kit asks when we lose the others on the next floor. "I saw that old lady hovering around."

"Although it's only one out of the many here, it feels good to have brought peace to both her and Olivia."

On the way home, Kit sits silently in the backseat, and I can almost feel her stewing about her predicament. Logan chats about the ceremony. "It'll be great to see so many gathered together at the vineyard. All of our friends and family. I missed your dad at the bachelor party."

"He said he wanted it to be just you, Chuck, and your friends. He thought you might feel stifled with him there. I hope he remembered to pick up his tux. I better check."

Logan reaches across the seat and stops me from calling him. "He wouldn't forget something like that. You're his shining star."

If only Logan realized how many events Daddy missed while I was growing up. Although he was a police officer in town for many years, his head was always full of song lyrics and guitar chords, and then because of our family curse, Mama forced him to leave. Music means everything to him, and he is often forgetful about the real world because he's inside his own.

But Logan is right, this is something he wouldn't forget. Besides, Mama will make sure everything goes as planned. Knowing her, she's written a speech for him to give at the reception.

For now, I squeeze Logan's hand and allow myself a moment of ease. Everything is going to be wonderful.

FIFTEEN

At The Wedding Chapel, I gather Rosie and Jenn and go down our checklist for Saturday. Logan heads to his office, Moxley on his heels, and Kit sits on the back porch.

I hear a familiar female voice as I mark off items on the list as Rosie and Jenn report in about what is finished, and what still needs to be done. I hope my great-grandmother has words of comfort, if not wisdom, for my friend.

There are only a few things left to complete, and most have to wait until tomorrow or Saturday. I'm relieved, but I still have the ghosts in the barn to get rid of, not to mention resolving whatever is going on with the pregnant one in my backyard. At the moment, however, I have a speech to practice and a dress to try on.

Upstairs, I remove the wedding gown from the garment bag and hang it on the back of the spare bedroom door. I run my fingers over the beautiful material and smile. It's perfect, from its lovely neckline to its delicate, detachable train. Gloria has done an outstanding job with every detail, including the slip of satin and lace at the bottom of the deep V in the back. It's a piece of fabric from the gown Mama and Aunt Willa shared that we added last week. Gloria blended it flawlessly with the satin so I can carry both of these strong, amazing women who've influenced my life with me down the aisle.

As a carrot to get in front of the mirror to practice, I hold off on slipping into it, allowing the anticipation to build. I angle my standing mirror—one of Aunt Willa's antiques—so I can see the dress hanging behind me. Hearing my voice is cringeworthy, but watching myself give the speech is even worse. I try to channel Mama and her confidence, along with her big, friendly smile. It looks too forced, which it is—maybe it's better if I don't stare at my reflection. "Hello, and welcome to Thornhollow's annual Fall Festival!"

The good thing is, halfway through, I realize I'm not even using my notes. I pace around, getting into the flow of what I want to convey. I love this town, love my heritage, and I mean every word of my speech. Walking helps me loosen up, and it's too bad I can't do that during the actual address.

By the time I finish, I've returned to the mirror and realize I don't need to channel Mama. There's enough of her already in me, and as long as I am sincere, which I am, it will naturally come through.

With my anticipation at a peak and my confidence high, I lay my notes on the dresser and gaze unabashedly at what Gloria has dubbed the *pièce de résistance.*

I am determined not to let anyone else see the gown before the ceremony. It's my greatest design, incorporating my favorite features. I even have a pocket hidden in the layers of the skirt for my lip gloss.

A cat claws at the door outside. It could just be Lancelot

or Arthur, or it could be Tabby. A twinge of guilt hits me when I ignore the meowing that follows. I love my great-grandmother dearly, but I'm keeping this under wraps until Saturday at the church. The scratch comes again, then a *pop* and my grandmother's voice. "Ye be all right in there, Avalon?"

As I suspected. "Right as rain," I tell her. "Did you enjoy your conversation with Kit?"

"She told me about the shadow cat, and Sage's thoughts on the matter."

I edge closer. I didn't lock it, and I feel her impatience on the other side. "Do you agree with her theory?"

"Be there a reason for us not to discuss this face-to-face?"

"Yes, I'm trying on my wedding gown."

The knob wiggles, and I grab it, keeping her from entering. "What's this, now?" she asks. "Let me see you."

"Not now. Saturday."

"I am your grandmother and matriarch of this family."

I rest my forehead on the wood. "And I appreciate you respecting my wishes."

Footsteps pound up the staircase. "Hey, Tabitha," Logan says, then to me, "Ava, we need to go soon."

"I'll be down shortly."

The two of them leave, talking in soft voices. Locking the door, I breathe a sigh of relief and trail my fingers over the dress once more. I slip out of my street clothes and into it, luxuriating in the soft rustle of the material.

It's a dream, wearing my own design. I can't keep the smile off my face as I draw the fabric up over my hips. I feel nearly—dare I think it?—bubbly. A tiny laugh escapes me. I slide my arms through the holes and adjust the top with its built-in support. Things are...tight. I make a few adjustments, but when I attempt to zip up the side opening, I only get halfway. I suck in my breath and try to reduce the size of my ribcage. No dice. The zipper refuses to move.

A small spark of panic hits me low in my belly. I unzip it, peel the dress down off my torso, and examine my naked self in the mirror. Have I gained weight? The fabric around my hips is definitely snugger than I anticipated, but I just had a fitting a week ago. I try again.

The zipper refuses to go past the halfway point, the bodice so tight it pushes a roll of skin up over it. I feel sick—I can't have gained that much weight since last week!

Worse, what if I'm... I take a deep breath and try to calm my racing pulse. "Okay, Ava, don't panic." I close my eyes for a brief second, unzip, and adjust the material around my hips. My fingers pause over the zipper, and I have to cheerlead myself into a third attempt. "Everything is fine. You can do this."

I finger the small zipper carefully, exhale all my breath, and pull in my ribs. Then I start the slow ascent of the metal teeth, one by one, feeling the fabric tighten around my ribcage.

"Ava!" Logan's voice makes my taut nerves jangle. "We need to go."

I swallow hard and tug, forcing it higher. The final half inch is out of reach, however, and I grunt and wrench at it some more.

Pointless. If I yank any more zealously, the zipper will break.

"Everything okay up there?"

It's most definitely *not*. In two days, I'm getting married, and my creation doesn't fit! I choke on a sob, unzip the side, and let the beautiful fabric pool at my feet. "Be right down," I call, disheartened.

I can't be pregnant; my last cycle finished only a few days ago. If anything, I should have lost the bloating that usually accompanies it.

Head spinning, and heart thumping with dread, I return the dress to its hanger inside the garment bag. After throwing my clothes on, I decide to talk to Gloria after the parade. I pray she'll know what to do.

Downstairs, the freak-out I'm having internally must show on my face. Logan assumes it's because of the speech. He takes me by the shoulders and looks me in the eye. "You're going to do great. Just be yourself."

I nod and follow him out the front door, Rosie and Kit accompanying us. Jenn tells us she'll see us there.

People, floats, and those riding in designated cars with banners are lining up in the church parking lot. The high school marching band is practicing in one corner, and fire trucks and police cars fill the street. Locals speak to us, wave, and there's a general lightheartedness to it all. Queenie has her usual table set up with refreshments, and she hands Logan a bag of cinnamon candies as we go by.

The podium on top of a hayrack on Main Street awaits me from its spot on a corner lawn. As we draw near, Mama catches my eye, waving frantically from the raised platform where she's testing the mic and speakers. Locals and tourists crowd both sides of the street, cordoned off at each end so no vehicles can get through, except for those in the parade. Children ride bikes, zoom past us on skateboards, and run amok, pure freedom egging them on. I smile at their exuberance, forgetting my troubles for a few minutes.

The quaint shops have their doors open, shoppers

roaming in and out, waiting for the festivities to begin. Kids in costumes skip by, some greeting me. When I reach the hayrack, Logan boosts me up and hands me off to Mama. She's wearing her favorite blue suit, her cheeks flushed. I kiss her on one of them and she gives me a pat on the back. Her excitement is hard not to catch. "Ava, isn't it wonderful? We estimate we've increased our attendance by several hundred folks."

"You and the Chamber always put on a wonderful festival."

She beams over the crowd. "We do, don't we? And we're adding the peanut jamboree next year. The council has given its approval, so we'll be having our inaugural kickoff in September. I'm so excited!"

She lives and breathes this stuff. "Congratulations. That's great news."

"What's wrong?" Her exuberance fades. "You look like someone stole your cat."

I debate telling her that my wedding dress doesn't fit. No point in ruining her day and making her worry. "Just focused on giving my speech. Trying to stay in my Zen mode."

An immaculate brow lifts, and I know she isn't buying it. "It's Helen, isn't it? Lordy, that woman!"

"No, not her. I haven't even spoken to her." This is the truth, although there are very few days when St. Helen isn't a challenge. "You go on and finish up. I'm going to review my notes."

On cue, the audio expert calls her over, and she squeezes my arm before she hustles to the microphone. They run through a sound check while I pat my pockets, searching for my speech.

Oh no! With a whole new sense of dread, I realize I left it at home. Checking my watch, the dread blooms larger. There's no time to retrieve it. I have to do this off the cuff.

I swallow hard, knees beginning to shake.

Logan is in the crowd across the street from me. He smiles and gives me a thumbs-up. Kit is on one side of him, Sage and Raven joining him on the other. Everything in my mind blanks out—except for pure panic.

"It's time, Ava," Mama calls. "We're about to start."

My feet feel frozen to the spot. I begin to speak, but no words come out. *Get it together, Ava.* I glance around at the dozens and dozens of faces watching me, spilling over the sidewalks and even staring down from the upper levels of the buildings. *They're counting on you.*

Forcing away my fear, I step forward to take her place at the podium as the audio guy plays a recording of our town song and folks sing along with it. When it ends, they cheer and clap.

The marching band and the lead floats have arrived. Mama now stands behind the banner strung across the front and held by two council members, ready to cut it when I end my welcome and kick off the parade. As the last of the clapping subsides, I glance over the masses, and spot Daddy. He stands on the elevated hill down the side street next to the flag pole.

But his attention isn't on me or Mama. I follow his gaze and my mouth goes dry. Howard and Drew Hurley are in the midst of those gathered. They're behind two tall men, as tall as Drew himself, but close enough to Kit to touch her.

While Howard stares at the back of her head with longing on his face, his son appears angry. His aura flares red and ripples, reminding me of crackling flames, and his eyes aren't right.

They're glowing green.

SIXTEEN

I step back, a new sense of panic setting in. The movement must capture his attention because his gaze shifts to me.

And then it's gone—his irises are normal, his face serene, almost bored.

I blink, wondering if it was the slant of the afternoon sun. More likely, it's my stress. For a single fluttery heartbeat, I consider calling Logan closer and whispering for him to get Kit out of here, to take her back to The Chapel, but then I realize this is actually the best place for her to be. She's surrounded by people, and no matter how much Drew hates her, he won't act on it in public.

Is he our culprit?

The crowd has fallen silent, all eyes on me, waiting. I shake myself out of my thoughts and restore my smile. I hope it reaches my eyes as I attempt to keep them on Drew and his father. The two men in front make that difficult, and I see Logan, frowning at me, when I scope the rest of the observers. Far in the rear, my dad is also frowning. When our eyes meet, he holds up both hands in question, seeming to ask, *what's wrong?*

Mama clears her throat loud enough to carry to the podium. *Yes, yes, all right.* "Hello and welcome to the kickoff of Thornhollow's annual Fall Festival!" They cheer. When that dies down, I smile wider and nod, my mouth dry, mind scrambling to remember the opening I so carefully practiced. "I'm Ava Fantome-Cross, president of the Chamber of Commerce, and today, you're in for a real treat."

A round of applause that gives me a breath to rack my memory. "Each year, we gather during this season to celebrate the final harvest of summer and the bounty we enjoy from our labors, and we're delighted to have you with us for today's parade."

A few folks whistle and clap, but I sense I'm already losing them, many eyes glancing toward Mama and her banner.

If only I hadn't forgotten my notes. My mind is blank, my focus shifting between Kit and Drew, whom I can no longer see. Are he and his father still here?

A kid dressed as a Marvel character yells, "When do we get candy?"

Laughter spills from the spectators. "Very soon." I clear my throat, considering using the moment to skip the rest of the speech that I can't remember anyway and get underway, but I know there are people I need to mention, activities I'm supposed to remind folks about, the plug for shopping downtown I'm required to squeeze in.

Persephone chooses that moment to appear at my elbow. I startle. "Check your pocket," she says.

"What?" Everyone is frowning and murmuring now. Of course, they can't see her. I appear to be talking to myself. But when I do as instructed and stick my hand in my pocket, there it is—my speech. An audible sigh of relief leaves my lips and I place the paper on the podium's top, smoothing out the wrinkles. A giddy laugh bubbles up in my throat.

She eyes the gawkers and sniffs. "You can thank me later." She disappears.

My legs tremble like they're made of jelly. I grip the sides of the wooden top, mimicking Reverend Stout on Sunday mornings. I've covered my opening well enough, so I drop to the meat of my address and start again. Every word I've practiced comes flowing back to me, and after a sentence or two, I look up to see I've captured people's attention again. I don't need my notes after that, except to be sure I don't miss acknowledging those who've worked diligently to pull this all off. "The farmer's market is tomorrow from eight to noon at the courthouse, Hildy's Hillbilly Band plays in that same spot from one to three, and the Treat the Street Event begins at four and runs until eight tomorrow night. It's five dollars per family and a dozen stores are participating. Every child in costume will receive treats."

Before I end, I pause, looking out on those I love, my neighbors, my friends. "Today is extra special to me," I tell them, "in so many ways. I owe my gratitude to this town and its citizens for welcoming me home, and for trusting me to take over where my Aunt Willa, who is still one of the greatest influences of my life, left off. I dedicate this Fall Festival to her memory." I glance skyward. "Aunt Willa, I hope you're happy where you are and proud of our town. I miss you. Watch over all of us this weekend, and give us your blessing."

A huge round of applause echoes up and down the street, folks whistling and cheering once more. Logan, Daddy, Kit, Sage, Raven, Rosie, and Jenn are all smiling and nodding at me. Daddy winks. Most importantly, Mama beams when I turn to her and the others gathered at the front of the procession.

I can see in her eyes she's proud of me, as well as the event. "Mayor Fantome," I call, holding out a hand toward her. All eyes turn to focus on her and the first float, excitement rippling in the air. "The Hulk over here needs his candy." Folks chuckle. "Do us the honor and get this party started!"

Ruckus cheers, clapping, hooting, and laughter rings out. Mama raises a hand and counts, "One, two, three!"

She cuts through the banner with a pair of giant scissors the Chamber uses for grand openings. She and the council members march forward and those who've spilled off the congested sidewalks jump back. The band plays, the floats begin their trek, and I step away from the podium, but remain on the hayrack, keeping an eye on Kit and Logan. It isn't easy, the jumbled mass of bodies shifting and weaving as people attempt a better view, and the taller floats obstructing mine.

Those riding on them and in the cars throw handfuls of candy, kids racing each other to grab as many pieces as possible. A few folks have dogs with them and random barks intertwine with the noisy atmosphere. Queenie, Brax, and Rhys stand off to one side of the gift shop and Queenie smiles at me.

After a float with a Halloween theme that includes a rickety castle tower made from foam and painted to mimic gray stones, passes by, I notice the men who stood a head taller than even Drew have moved down the block to a different spot. Howard and Drew are no longer there and I scan the rows of tightly packed spectators, searching for them. At least they're nowhere near Kit.

While their dislike of her is one thing, I now believe I should have taken it more seriously. I still can't get the image of Drew's eyes out of my head. Did I imagine it? Was it another hallucination?

Anticipating the end, I fidget, needing to cross the street and talk to Sage and Raven. I feel a tingling sensation at the nape of my neck like earlier at the Cross mansion. Sure enough, I've been so worried about Kit and my speech, that I've tuned out the spirit world. Unfortunately, it hasn't tuned me out. Dozens of ghosts float over the grounds, passing right through people, buildings, and the floats. How rude.

I grit my teeth and manage to catch Sage's attention. I signal for her to meet me behind Sweet Cicely's, a gift shop with an eclectic bohemian vibe. She nods and once the last car in the parade rolls by at a snail's pace, I step off the platform and wait for Logan and Kit to reach me.

"That was great," he says. "Nice add about Willa."

Kit cuts her eyes to the left and right. "You see all those spirits hanging around?"

"Fairly normal with big crowds," I say. "Plenty of folks have loved ones clinging to them."

She shivers. "I've never noticed so many in a single place before. Gives me the creeps. You don't think it's due to... me?"

"Gives me the creeps, too, but I don't think it's connected to you," I reply. "Sorry, but I need to talk to Mama and apologize for my stumbling start. Logan, can you take Kit to her next appointment?"

A crease appears in the center of his forehead. "Sure." He sounds tentative about leaving me. "Was a ghost bugging you on stage?"

"Persephone, but she figured out I left my speech at home and somehow magically stuck it in my pocket."

His worry turns to surprise. "Impressive. I suspect she's capable of a lot more than we give her credit for."

Scary thought, that.

My dad emerges from the fading crowd. "Hey, sweetie." He hugs me. "You did well today."

I appreciate that they're all attempting to buoy my spirits. "A little shaky at first, but I come from strong stock." I wink. "I recovered and persevered."

It's something he and Mama have preached to me my whole life. Daddy pats my arm and smiles. "I'm proud of you."

It was a simple speech, nothing particularly noteworthy, yet I feel warm and happy hearing his and Logan's praise. "Thanks. I appreciate it. I'm not comfortable being on stage like that, and although I pulled it off this time, I think I'll leave future oratory opportunities to others." I need to find Sage, but I remember to ask about his tux.

"Ready and waiting for my stroll down the aisle."

Logan and Kit leave for the hospital, and once they're out of hearing range, I lower my voice. "Do you know Dr. Howard Hurley?"

His brows dip. "Should I?"

"You were watching him and his son, Drew."

"Drew Hurley. I thought that was him. Watched him play college ball some years back. Now, he's gone professional. He's good."

"Ever hear anything negative about him?"

Daddy's frown deepens. "Not that I recall. Why?"

"It's nothing." I hope. "Logan's been offered a temporary teaching position at the college next spring. He used to play on the same team with Drew. I have a funny feeling about him and a situation that involves Kit. I might be paranoid, but I'm worried about his intentions."

There's a lot left unsaid in all that, and yet my father gets the gist. "Want me to look into his background?"

"You read my mind." Although he's no longer on the force, Daddy has connections. "Could you?"

Mama is bustling toward us, being stopped every few yards by someone wanting to praise or criticize the festival, or possibly her leadership. The life of a politician. It happens everywhere she goes. "Anything for you," Daddy says.

There's a young male ghost hovering near, acting impatient. He's going to talk to me, whether I want him to or not, so I kiss Daddy on the cheek. "Tell Mama I'm sorry and I'll call her later."

I scurry to the alley next to Sweet Cicely's, the hovering ghost following me. "He's watching you, you know."

"Who?"

"Bigfoot."

At first, I figure he's simply a whacky fellow. Then it clicks. With a sharp pivot, I whirl to look behind me. Drew is fast, but not before I catch a glimpse of his orange shirt disappearing around the corner. I charge after him, not a clue what I might say if I catch up to him, but rounding the building, I discover he's vanished.

There are a dozen stores he might have slipped into and I ask the ghost, "Which way did he go?" but he's gone, too. I'm aiming for the nearest shop door when Sage intercepts me,

Raven by her side. "I thought you wanted to talk to us," Sage says.

At war with myself over what to do, I reluctantly give up the idea of a chase. "Drew and his father—I think something is going on with them and their connection to Kit."

"How did her CT scan go?" Raven asks.

"We don't know anything yet, but I saw something odd while I was on the podium."

Sage glances at some women as they pass us, drawing me into the alley and lowering her voice. "A ghost?"

"Well, a whole lot of those, but that's not what I'm talking about. It's Drew. He was staring at Kit during my speech and he looked...weird."

Raven frowns. "The basketball player?"

I nod. "His eyes glowed." The sisters exchange a glance and then stare at me, waiting for more. I shift out of a patch of sunlight. "Maybe it was the sun reflecting off him, or the stress of this weekend really is getting to me and I hallucinated it."

"You're *not* hallucinating." Sage pats my arm. "Did the world go monochrome when it happened?"

"Nope." Another pair of women pass, talking and laughing brightly, two children in tow. "Everything was perfectly normal."

The sisters look at each other again, some form of silent communication passing between them. "We saw Logan leave with Kit," Sage says. "Want us to walk you home?"

We'll have more privacy to discuss all this "woo-woo" stuff, as Mama often calls it. I can see they also believe it's best not to leave me alone. "That would be great."

"I enjoyed your speech," Raven says as we cross through the church parking lot.

The last of the floats have completed their trip and arrived back here to be torn down, another fall parade in the books. Kids chase around and holler to each other, the band members tucking away instruments and those in charge of the various committees calling out orders.

"Thanks," I say. "Standing in front of people and speaking isn't my jam."

She chuckles. "Good thing you had an angel looking after you."

Persephone. I owe her. "You saw her?"

"Mostly just the magical aura around her."

That reminds me... "Drew had a strange aura today. And his father seemed like he's still pining after Kit, even though he claims otherwise."

"What do you mean by strange?" Sage asks. "I'm afraid in our world, that covers a lot of ground."

"Red and orange flames. It seemed to crackle with them." I notice Raven's expression and wonder if I'm wrong, but plunge in anyway. "I don't typically see them, and I'm no expert, but that's jealousy and anger, isn't it?"

"Most certainly." We wait for a passing vehicle before stepping off the sidewalk and crossing the street to the rear of the tea shop. "He's carrying a vendetta."

"Yes, but is he psychic?" Sage looks doubtful. "Especially one who's strong enough, and versed in magic, to create such a spell on Kit?"

"I don't know him, Logan does, but he hasn't seen Drew in years. A lot could have changed since they were schoolmates. I have my dad running a background check on him. Even if he's not the source of Kit's problem, he obviously has a lot of anger over what happened between his parents and blames her. I want to know if he's acted out previously when he's been upset. The look he gave her rang all of my warning bells, flaming aura or not. I don't want us so focused on our psychic attacker that we miss one who might do her physical harm."

We pause at the side of the tea shop, the few parking spaces filling already with customers. "You know," Raven says, "that much rage can be its own kind of power. It can create its own thought form, plaguing its target with mental health issues."

A group of older women exit a Buick, waving and calling to Sage. They're dressed in long skirts, capes, and flamboyant earrings. I've seen them before when they come for readings and workshops on white and green witchcraft. She returns their greetings. "Be right there!"

Lia comes racing up behind us, out of breath. "I've got it," she exclaims, leaping onto the low porch. She pulls a set of keys from her pocket and welcomes the ladies inside.

"Lia's helping you?" I ask.

Sage gives a one-shoulder shrug. "She needs money for some trip she wants to take to a haunted museum in Biloxi."

Why am I not surprised Lia wants to visit some creepy place reported to be haunted? Like we don't have enough ghosts roaming Thornhollow. "So it's possible Drew could be behind Kit's problem simply because of his hatred of her? What about the shadow cat? His eyes glowed green, just like that ghost familiar's."

Raven crosses her arms in contemplation and fingers the triquetra pendant hanging around her neck. "All I'm saying is that it could be a contributing factor. We need more information."

"I'm closing at five," Sage says. "We'll hit the library after that. Will you be okay until Logan gets home?"

"Yes." I have calls to make and a dress to squeeze into. "Rosie and Jenn will be there shortly, and my grandmother is always around."

I leave them and cross to The Wedding Chapel, already dialing Gloria's number.

SEVENTEEN

"Should I come now, *chérie?*" Gloria is as upset as I am. "I don't understand how this could happen! Everything fit perfectly last week!"

"I'm afraid I must've put on a few pounds. I'm not sure how it happened." I should have asked Sage for a tea to eliminate fluid. I'm sure she has something that could help. "I don't plan on eating anything until the reception now."

Gloria *tsks*. Her normally light, French accent becomes heavier. "*Non!* You must eat. We can't have you passing out during your vows."

"I have something I have to do this evening. Maybe you could come first thing in the morning?" Hopefully, she can adjust the seams and give me a little more space. Between that and my crash diet, I *am* going to fit in that dress on Saturday. "I'm so sorry about this."

"We will fix it," she insists. "Do not worry."

We say our goodbyes. Next, I text Sage. *Do you have any tea that helps you lose weight? Quickly*, I add.

While I wait for her reply, I text Winter. I'm on a roll.

Hello, my friend. I have a question regarding a new development with my abilities. Do you have time for a quick chat?

Winter responds before Sage, even though she's several time zones away. The phone rings, and I answer, smiling. "That was quick."

She chuckles. "Spring has me harvesting gourds in the garden. It's either that or stand behind the register at the shop this afternoon. I'd rather be outside than with people." She makes a disgusted tone in the back of her throat. "A chat with you is the perfect break. What's up?"

I wish you could be here for our wedding. I almost say it before I launch into what's been going on, but I know it will only make her feel bad. She and her sisters have a busy life, running their metaphysical shop and offering healings to people. Winter is a medium, like me, and she has made it part of her career, bringing peace to those still living, while helping those who've transitioned find closure.

Unlike me, she enjoys it.

I give her a brief rundown of events, mentioning the time riding. "Have you ever experienced anything like that? Do you know about the space between dimensions where ghosts hang out?"

"Fractured pieces of time can get caught, just like the spirits who are tied here. From what I know, it's uncommon for the living to be able to access that dimension, but anything is possible. My mother always claimed that the Earth holds certain memories and projects them over and over again, like an old movie reel onto a screen. That's often what we're tapping into when we see loops of the past. They're broken fragments that slip over our current one. Could that be what happened? You stepped into her broken time-space continuum?"

"Sure sounds like it, but this ghost interacted with me. It wasn't a time loop. She was cognitive, just stuck in a broken fragment, I guess. She doesn't realize she had her baby and died. She can't go back and she can't move forward. I'm not even sure she *can* cross to the afterlife."

She's quiet a moment, thinking it over. "That in-between space defies normal laws of physics. Pretty radical stuff."

It's said with a bit of teasing. "You know me, always pushing the boundaries. Do you have any suggestions for how I can stop it? Persephone seems to think it's a bad idea."

"It's absolutely a bad idea. You could get stuck there, or interact there in one spot, and come out somewhere else, like in front of a bison, on a deserted island, on a street in New York with a bus bearing down on you, or something even worse. Time fragments are random and chaotic. There's no guarantee that you'll get dumped out where you went in. Let me talk to my sisters and Mamma Nightingale. I'll get back to you, okay?"

I'd hoped for an immediate plan of action, but as with all these things, research was needed. "Is there a crystal or spell that can keep me here in this time-space reality? Even if it's temporary?"

"You need to stay as connected and grounded to the Earth as you can. Use black and red crystals, stay centered, meditate. Anything that keeps you present and mindful. Keep away from the gazebo, maybe even your backyard for now. It goes without saying, but avoid places that have potential spirits."

"Sure, no problem. That's super easy."

She chuckles at the sarcasm in my voice. "I know you're getting married on Saturday, but is there any way you could remain at home, inside, for now until I figure this out? I know you have the house warded and spelled. That's the safest spot for you. If you have to go out, take your black kyanite and that iron cross you have. That should keep the spirits at bay, but no guarantees."

"I'll do my best."

"How are the preparations coming, by the way?"

I'm facing the dress on the back of the door, cozy in its garment bag. I want to bring it out and try it on again. There has to be a mistake; like Gloria said, last week, it fit perfectly. I move it to the closet and eye myself in the mirror. "Tomorrow is a big day. We have to decorate the church and we have the rehearsal and dinner."

"This ghost sure picked a weird time to show. Wonder what triggered her to reach out now?"

I give her the background about Nettie and Bobby V while searching for my bag filled with supplies for warding off ghosts. "I think we've stirred things up. What are the odds that she would end up buried in my backyard?"

"You're in quite a pickle."

"What's new?" It's my turn to laugh, tucking the kyanite blade in my skirt pocket. "If I could just cross her, I imagine it would resolve a lot. Or maybe if I crossed her mother..."

"Were you not listening to what I just said? You have to stay away from them. I know you want to help every spirit that intersects your path, but they need to wait until we figure out how to keep you safe while you do it."

She's right. The iron cross is heavy in my palm. I rub my thumb over it. "I wasn't going to say this, because I certainly don't want you to feel any pressure, but I sure wish you were here. Not only to help me with this mess, but because I miss you. I never dreamed I'd have a big ceremony and you wouldn't be with me."

"I'll get on my broom and fly there now."

Winter always knows how to make me smile and it's good to see my reflection lighten. "Too bad you can't use these fractured pieces of time to pop over."

"You tell Persephone she needs to step up and assist you with this. She's a guardian angel, emphasis on guardian. There has to be something she can do to protect you from accidentally slipping into these cracks."

Persephone was originally Winter's spirit guide. "Honestly, I'd rather have you by my side. Although, she did help me earlier. I forgot my speech for the parade and she brought it to me."

Speaking of... I feel something tug on a strand of my hair, and the angel in question appears behind me, scowling. "You are so ungrateful," she says.

I stick my tongue out at her while I tell Winter, "Thanks for calling. I can't tell you how much I appreciate you and your advice."

"I'll get back to you as soon as I can. Hang in there."

We disconnect and I turn to Persephone. "Winter says you can help me with this time-riding issue. I need protection so I don't accidentally end up in New York City in front of a bus."

She leans against the dresser, giving me a confused look. "That makes no sense."

I relay what Winter told me. "I don't want to get lost in the time-space continuum."

"Do you really think I would let that happen?"

Maybe. "I need reassurance that you won't."

She scowls. "I promise."

Why don't I feel better? "Did you and Sherlock have any luck with Nettie?"

"Until she's accepted that she's dead, we're not going to. Sherlock tried everything." She shrugs, palms up. "She's a stubborn one."

"How do we get her to cooperate?"

She taps her finger against her cheek. "I'm not sure. If you could get her and Maria Grace so they could see each other, you might be able to cross them at the same time."

"How do I do that? Get them together?"

"Did you notice that shrine Nettie had? There's some energy in that. I wonder if you could use it like a magnet to draw the girl's spirit to her mother's room."

That makes sense. "If Maria Grace's body is under the gazebo, can it go that far from her remains?"

Some earthbound spirits are tied to their bones, keeping them near the site of their burial. Others are connected to the place it happened, especially if it was an unexpected death, such as a murder or an accident. They can only travel so far before they're snapped back to whatever is anchoring them here. "You've only spoken to the girl in the in-between dimension. She may not be as tied here as you think."

Hope rises in my chest. "How do I do it? Call her to her mother's altar?"

Another casual shrug. "A seance should work."

Great. I'm sure Helen will love that. Still, that's more than I had before. I remember Winter's warning, but this could work, and I have the kyanite and cross to keep me anchored. "I'll round up my usual posse and try it tomorrow." Maybe she or Sage will have more insight on keeping me from ending up on a desert island by then. "You'll be there?"

"Wouldn't miss it."

"I want Sherlock, too. Both of you should come to the library tonight, as well, and lend a hand with our research."

She gives a dismissive wave. "I'll let him know." She disappears in the blink of an eye.

"I do appreciate you," I call to the empty room, knowing she's still listening. "Thank you for earlier with my speech, and with the seance idea."

My hair flips again, this time good-naturedly.

I think.

EIGHTEEN

I make a point to text Winter and tell her Persephone's suggestion, as much as to smooth things over with the angel by giving her the credit—I know she reads my messages and eavesdrops on calls—as to get Winter's thoughts.

Downstairs, I hear the front door open, and the sound of Logan and Kit's voices. Logan calls my name. Heading for the steps, I raise my voice. "Be right down."

A reply comes from Sage. *Why are you going on a diet? You don't need to lose weight.*

Apparently, I do. *My dress doesn't fit,* I type out.

It's tough for me to admit it, even to her. My thumb hovers over the Send button as Logan comes into view at the bottom of the stairs. I swallow my pride and tap it.

"Are you sick?" he asks.

I hustle down on bare feet, wiping away the consternation from my face. "Not at all. How was the appointment?"

He brushes a light kiss across my lips and leads me to the

kitchen. "Pretty much the same as the previous— She was in and out in a few minutes, but no one told her anything."

Kit has her head in our fridge. "I need food. What do you have to eat?"

She's a bottomless pit. Another response dings from Sage. I excuse myself to let them rustle up dinner. She doesn't comment about my weight gain, only says, *I'll bring you something.*

With all these witchy women in my life, along with the finest seamstress in the South, surely one of them can get me into my gown. The tension in my neck and shoulders eases a bit. I glance through some stuff on my desk and then return to find Logan and Kit putting together salads and heating soup.

"We voted for quick and easy," Kit tells me.

"I'm not hungry," I fib. "But I *am* tired." It smells good and my stomach protests, grumbling loudly. "I'm going to lie down for a few minutes before we go to the library."

Logan scans my face. "Are you sure you're not sick?"

"Positive." I get three feet from the stairs before he catches me. "We have to keep up your strength for the big day." He winks. "And our honeymoon. I'll bring you a tray."

I caress his cheek. "Thank you for taking care of me, but that's not necessary."

"I'll make you a cup of tea," he suggests.

Sage has impeccable timing. She and Lia arrive just then. "Raven is closing." She crosses the foyer and hands me a pale yellow paper bag. "This will help."

"Help what?" Logan asks.

I hesitate. "Girl stuff."

His eyes widen, and he turns away. "Gotcha. Anyone hungry?"

Lia bobs on the balls of her feet. "Me! Me!"

She tags after him. Sage fingers the strap of her messenger bag before removing it from her shoulder and setting it on Rosie's desk. "What's going on with the dress?"

I lower my voice. "It was fine last week. Now, it's too tight. I can't zip it."

She pinches my bicep, sizing it up. "You don't look like you've gained any weight."

I don't feel like it either. "I must have. How fast does this tea work?"

"Drink four ounces every two hours and you'll drop several pounds overnight."

I open the bag and look inside, the aroma of various herbs and spices filling my nose. It smells a lot like licorice and I grimace. Not my favorite. "Between this and Gloria's magic hands, I have to get in my gown and not resemble a walrus in a tutu."

"A word to the wise—diuretics such as this can cause dehydration. If we had more time, I'd suggest a full body cleanse, but those work over several days. This is quicker, but also slightly risky."

"Can you spell me into thinness?"

She coughs a laugh. "If I could, I'd be a millionaire."

Logan calls from the kitchen, "Water's hot."

"Be right there," I reply.

"Why didn't you tell him?" she whispers.

"He's already worried enough about me. I'm going to have to be extra sneaky about not eating."

"I don't recommend fasting."

"I know, I know." I head for the kitchen. "Can't say I'm looking forward to it."

With everyone watching me, I end up accepting a salad

and moving it around a lot with my fork, but consuming little. The tea does, in fact, taste like licorice and it's hard to choke it down. I keep the image of my perfect wedding in my head for motivation.

Raven joins us once she's finished at the shop, and she alerts Paris, one of the librarians, about our visit. After we're done, and I am rinsing the dishes before loading them into the washer, I glance through the window and see the faint outline of a spirit. I ignore it.

Logan takes Moxley out to do his business. Kit runs to the bathroom and Lia chats with her mom on her cell. She gets permission to go with us, and I am so worried about my dress, Kit, and how to get the ghosts out of my way by three on Saturday, I don't even care.

She hangs up, giddy that she gets to help us with our research. "I'm kicking off my podcast with your ceremony," she tells me, grabbing a soda from the fridge. "Also, I'm starting a blog for your website. We're going to highlight bridal clients and their experiences. It's going to be awesome!"

I stick the last two glasses into the top rack. "Sorry, what?"

"I haven't decided on a name yet. Happily Ever After Wedding Tales. The Brides of Thornhollow." Her eyes gleam with a far-off vision. "A Walk Down The Aisle. Wedding Bells and Bridal Tales." She digs out her phone, her fingers racing over the keyboard. "Oooh, I like that one."

"A podcast? A blog?"

She clasps the device to her chest, and says dreamily, "Just think how much clients will love it."

They probably will, but... "You have time for all of this?" I sure don't.

"Why not?"

"You have school and extracurriculars. You have book-keeping for me, and now you're helping at the teashop."

"I know, right? I'm too lit to quit."

I laugh and hug her. "You are that, my young friend."

Outside, Moxley barks. I peek through the window. He's eyeing the older male ghost hovering around the edge of the gazebo.

Lia sidles up next to me, searching the yard. "What's he barking at?"

"Nothing."

She recognizes my tone. "Can I get my equipment?"

Putting a hand on her arm, I stop her. The ghost has seen me and waves, frantic for me to come out. I shake my head. Both at him and her. "No ghost hunting. We have to get to the library."

Logan cajoles Moxley to come, but he plants his chubby feet and growls menacingly toward the visitor. Logan has to pick the heavy dog up and carry him into the house. "I don't know what's gotten into him."

"Who knows?" I firm my lips as the ghost flails his arms again. "I'll lock up. You round up the others."

"I'll help," Lia says. "I'm going, too."

Logan sets Mox down and searches for his keys in his pocket. "You ride with Sage. You and Kit."

"Why?" I ask.

He gives me a knowing look. "Because I need time alone with my wife."

Busted. Lia runs off with her soda, giggling, and he leaves me standing there, giving the still-growling Moxley a pat on the head. "Is Tabby coming?"

"I haven't seen her." And I'm not about to walk down to the farmhouse to recruit her.

"You seem to be doing better, but if you don't feel up to going, you can stay and rest. I'll go with them and report back."

"That salad hit the spot. I'm good to go. Plus, I want to stay close to you."

A lopsided grin covers his face. "Not sick of me yet?"

I move in and wrap my arms around his neck. "I always feel better when I'm near you."

The grin grows and soon we're kissing. Lia whistles and we break apart, both of us grinning. "I'll be right there," I tell him. "I need to feed Arthur and Lancelot." Mox huffs. "And you, too," I tell him.

He pats the dog and walks out. I quickly feed the pets and step onto the porch. The house's wards include this space. "What do you want?" I ask quietly.

"She needs you." He glances around nervously. "I've done what I can for her, but it's not enough."

"Who? Maria Grace?"

He makes an exasperated gesture with his hands. "It was an accident. I tried to help."

"Help with what? If you want me to do something for her, you need to tell me what happened. Why she's here."

"She needed a place to hide. I knew it was a bad idea, but I let her stay in my barn. She went into labor. I couldn't save her, only the baby. I'm a doctor. *Was*, anyway."

"The baby lived?" I wonder if we're talking about the same woman.

He nods. "She needs closure with her mother. You have to help."

It feels like moving chess pieces around on a board.

Logan has tried to teach me the game, but I am horrible at it. "How did she end up buried under my gazebo?"

"Here?" His forehead knits in confusion as he points at the structure he's hiding behind. "She's not buried here."

This could be good news or worse news. "Where, then?"

His eyes dart across the lawn and hedge. His chin cocks at the B&B. "Why?"

Maybe it doesn't matter, but I want to know in case we have to dig her up and move her remains. She should be buried properly. "Not at your place?"

"This was my place. That house sits on the exact site of the barn."

I hesitate a moment. "She's under the house?"

"She was an unmarried, pregnant woman. It's not like she could be buried on sacred ground. I did the best I could for her."

He sounds sincere. There's just something...off about this. My mind flashes to her gasping, scared, at whatever spirit she saw behind me. It had to be him. "Did you know who the father was?"

"Not then. She refused to say. I'd seen her around, but didn't know her or her family."

Moving the gazebo to get to her bones is one thing. I can't do that to an entire house, nor ask my friends to in order to give her peace. Summoning her to her mother's shrine it is. "Are you related to me? That ground was part of the family acreage once."

"A very distant cousin," he claims. "I had the gift, you know."

"Doesn't feel like much of a gift to me." I wish Tabitha was here to confirm, or deny, his story. Where was she back when all this went down? "How did you get mixed up with Maria Grace?"

"She was having problems with the pregnancy. I was one of the few she trusted who would even talk to her."

"And why are you hanging around? Because you feel guilty about what happened?"

He gives me a shy smile and shakes his head. "I'm not an earthbound spirit."

"Then what are you?"

"I'm her guardian angel."

That certainly puts a different spin on things. Maybe that's what I was picking up on, yet... "Mine is much more physical in appearance. You look like a ghost. She didn't say anything about you, either. Does Persephone not know other guardian angels?"

"I don't really know how it works. I've been here a long time with Maria. She's the only charge I've ever had."

I wonder if the fact she's a spirit makes it harder, or perhaps, easier. "I think I have an idea about how to reunite her with her mother and get both of them to cross to the afterlife. I may need your help, though."

Relief passes over his features. "Anything. Let me know. The two of us have been hanging around far too long."

I feel trust flowing between us. "Why didn't you make your presence known to me sooner? I bet you have a lot of cool stories about my ancestors."

"I've never been able to connect with the previous mediums in our line. And with you, only in the past few days. You must be special." He glances at the farmhouse and back to me. "Not even Tabitha realized we were here. I'd love to chat about the family, but once Maria moves on, I'm not sure I'll get the chance."

Kit's voice filters to me from the entryway. "Ava? Are you coming?"

"I have to run," I say to him. "Thanks for your help. I'll let you know as soon as I have a solid plan in place to help your charge."

He disappears. I'm not sure I believe all of his story, but, regardless, I have to act on what he's told me.

NINETEEN

On the drive to the library, Logan is unnaturally quiet. "You can tell me anything, you know."

I don't want to keep him in the dark any longer. This is my life—*our* life. Yes, he'll worry, but he's already concerned, and not knowing the specifics about what's upsetting me only makes it worse. Besides, I feel more confident now that I have a plan for handling Maria Grace, as well as fitting into my dress.

Staying as unemotional as I can and sticking to the facts, I lay out all of it as we wind our way through the countryside. "The only thing I don't have a clue how to fix yet is Kit's predicament. Hopefully, Raven and Sage will discover a solution tonight. Just be prepared, because it may involve Drew."

His silence stretches out for a good half mile, but I give him a chance to process it all. "Divide and conquer," he finally says.

"What?"

"You handle the ghosts, I'll take Drew, and the witches will protect Kit."

He makes it sound easy. Straightforward.

Maybe it is. "And Gloria and the tea will get me into my gown."

His pretty blue eyes slide to mine. "I know how important the dress is to you, but as far as I'm concerned, you can wear a gunnysack and I'll still consider you the most beautiful woman in the room. I'm just relieved you're not sick."

I know this, yet hearing it hits me like a sack of Sage's crystals. I want to wear my gown because I designed it and it's been a dream of mine since I was a kid sketching in a notebook. But the fact of the matter is that I've gotten swept up in the *idea* of it—all of it. This huge ceremony to make his mother happy, and also my own need to prove to the town that I'm good enough for him. I lean across the shifter, laying my head on his shoulder. "Thank you. Is this why they call you Dauntless?"

He pats my thigh and chuckles. "I was raised by St. Helen."

'Nuff said.

I'd love for everything to go off perfectly, but this is me we're talking about. It's pure fantasy to think that's going to happen. "I promise that even if I can't wear my creation, I won't embarrass your mother in front of all her friends. I'll find something appropriate."

He chuckles and rubs the back of my head, massaging gently. "A noble quest. I'll do my best to assist you, my fair lady, simply because I don't want to hear Mother lament about it for the rest of her life."

It feels like a pact between us, and I smile to myself. He and I are blessed with formidable women for mothers. Their shadows are long and challenging to step out of. Yet, neither of us is intimidated by it, and we truly want them to be happy, just not at the expense of our happiness.

The library is dark when we arrive, the door locked. Sage leads us to the side and Paris greets everyone. She wears her dark brown hair up, her eyes dancing with mischief. "Ava, it's been a while. Good to see you. London sends her regards. She's out of town again."

I introduce her to Logan, Kit, and Lia. My intern instantly sets her sights on the kittens near the desk. They are the same as those that were here at my previous visit. Magical cats? Why not?

Paris takes us downstairs, and we leave Lia to play with them. We enter the secret, underground library dedicated to witches and wizards. Sherlock waves from his favorite table —this is where I first met him.

A year ago when I answered Aunt Willa's summons to return to Thornhollow, I hadn't even acknowledged my mediumship. The history and depth of the magical community in this area had been truly shocking for me when my search for ways to break a curse led me here.

Paris' grandmother, Iula, hovers her spectral body between two units of tall shelving, adjusting her glasses as she reads various titles. "I might have another for you," she calls.

Paris motions to the stack on the conference table. "Perhaps you could pause in your search for a moment, Meemaw, and say hello to our guests."

Her grandmother responds with a slight start, only now realizing we're here. Sherlock hops up from the desk. "I don't know where Persephone is. She's supposed to come and do that thing"— he makes a waving motion with his hand—"to make me visible. It should work on Iula, too."

She floats toward us, smiling, her hands raised in their usual palms-up pose that suggests a state of surprise or possibly readiness. I can never be sure which. "Is this your young man?" she asks me, peering at Logan over the frames of her spectacles.

Persephone appears at that moment, wearing a bright turquoise and orange outfit. Large toucan earrings sway from her earlobes. "I'm here, I'm here."

I indicate those gathered. "We could use some of your mojo so everyone can see Sherlock and Iula."

She snaps her fingers twice and Logan, not realizing Sherlock is standing next to him, startles and grabs at his chest. "Hey, man," he says, recovering. "Good to see you again. Literally."

Paris introduces her grandmother, and I do the same with Kit before getting down to business. "Have you run into this kind of spell before?" I ask. "Anything with ghost familiars?"

Once again, Paris points to the stack of books. "Through the years, we've heard of powerful psychics who have delved into this form of magic, but the last known in this area died twenty years ago. We've pulled all of the histories that mention her, along with the other magic users who dabbled in it, dating back to the 1700s."

Raven takes a seat and grabs the top volume. "At least it's a starting point."

For the next few hours, we dig in, reading and rereading entries, comparing notes, and flagging pages. Persephone suggests we trace the lineage of the last psychic witch,

Brianna Triste, and Iula brightens. "Yes, of course. That is a solid idea."

Persephone flicks a conceited look at Sherlock. "Me? Have a good idea? Who would believe it."

He rolls his eyes.

"How will that help us?" I ask.

"Psychic abilities run in families," Iula answers. "Tracking down her siblings, children, and any blood relations still living, could provide us with suspects."

Kit glances up from her compendium. "But wouldn't the library know if one of them was practicing magic?"

Iula raises a finger. "Not if he or she is using the spirit familiar to cloak it. In essence, that spell doesn't exist in the material world, only the ghostly one."

The things I learn.

"Isn't it possible, then, that Brianna could be spelling Kit from *that* world?" Logan inquires. All of our gazes go to him. He shrugs. "If the ghost familiar can channel a witch's power, why can't that power originate from a ghost itself?"

Sherlock smacks the table. "Brilliant deduction, my boy."

"A psychic ghost witch?" Kit shakes her head in disbelief. "Could this get any weirder? I didn't know this Brianna, and I'm sure I haven't met her spirit. What would she have against me?"

Paris sorts through the volumes in her stack and tugs one out. "I believe this mentioned that she occasionally offered her services for hire?"

"Yes." Iula claps her hands. "She did it all—swayed elections, struck down people's enemies, sold fertility charms, you name it."

Kit stares at her dumbfounded. "You're suggesting someone hired her ghost to attack me from the grave."

Neither Paris nor Iula seem surprised.

Even Raven is nodding, as if this makes sense. "It's possible. More likely if there is a go-between."

Her sister seems to catch on. "A living vessel, who doesn't have to have magical abilities, only a connection through her blood."

I sit back, also latching onto the thread of their theory. "A living relative summoned Brianna and forced her to do their bidding in order to attack Kit."

Raven flips pages. "Not only Kit. They might be using Brianna to make money by continuing to sell her services. Especially if they have no inherent abilities themselves, yet want to profit from hers."

For an expectant moment, we sit in silence, digesting the possibilities. Kit clears her throat, closing her book. "So we start with her relatives and that will most likely lead us to who hired him or her."

Sage takes out her phone. "Give me some names. Let's see if we can find anyone local."

Paris grabs the thick ancestry volume and finds the entry she wants. As she rattles off descendants, one jumps out at me. A cousin of Brianna's.

All the color bleeds from Kit's face. "Wait." She glances at me, Logan. "That can't be, can it?"

Paris glances up. "You know him?"

Logan has gone very still. "My whole life. He's not..."

Kit waves her hand over the collection of volumes. "Into all this? Apparently, he may be."

"We assume innocence until proven otherwise," Sherlock insists, seeing the shock and distress on our faces. To me, he adds, "I'll quiz Nettie. She might have witnessed or heard something that can give you leverage when you speak to him."

I nod and he disappears. He's right—jumping to conclusions won't help. Still, it's all I can do not to give in to my growing anger.

"He played me," Kit says so softly I almost don't hear it. My heart hurts for her. "Oh, Winston." She shakes her head. "I thought you were a good guy."

Logan's disbelief turns to rage. He grits his teeth, gripping the edge of the table. "He played us all."

"How do you know him?" Iula asks.

"He's been an employee of my family since I was born." I squeeze Logan's hand and he returns it, but a muscle ticks in his jaw. "His family has a long history with mine."

I hadn't realized that. "That's how he knew so much about Nettie."

"Who is she?" Paris asks.

I explain and she and Iula nod in unison. "Be careful," Iula says. "He may be keeping Nettie as a channel to Brianna. Nettie may not even realize it."

Her granddaughter adds, "Or she might be in on it. Especially since she doesn't want to leave the mortal realm. They're both getting something out of the arrangement, and if you attempt to sever it..." She gives me a disquieting look.

"What?" I ask, sure I don't want to know.

"All manner of ills could happen."

TWENTY

Prior to leaving, we briefly discuss the time-riding incidents, Logan becoming increasingly concerned when no one has any better ideas about controlling this new addition to my abilities than Winter. I keep the cross with me, my fingers smelling like the iron from rubbing it so much, even after I wash them. Back inside the house, I feel safer, but I can't stay here forever.

Logan offers to get me a glass of wine, but I feel like I'm floating away on tea and beg off our nightly ritual in front of the fireplace. Upstairs, he's asleep before I have time to broach the matter concerning Bobby V and his boss. Sherlock has confirmed that the two male ghosts in the barn are indeed our gangsters. Since they're hanging around the speakeasy, it's probable that they died nearby, or are buried within the vicinity. More bones to track down.

My bladder insists on being relieved every ten minutes. In order not to wake Logan or Moxley, the two of them snoring in a competitive manner as if it were the Olympics, I creep downstairs and into my office. Kit is sleeping in a spare bedroom, and we dropped Lia at home. The place is quiet and I'm grateful.

Going over my to-do list soothes my nerves. One more full day to go, and the list is long, but this is what I do—event planning. Weddings are my specialty. I've got this.

In between bathroom runs, Persephone drops in. She seems distracted and I assume she and Sherlock are still on the outs. Their romantic relationship is a roller coaster that speeds around far too fast for me to keep up with.

Sensing she wants me to ask, I start to, and she glares at me. I raise my hands in surrender. "You know, if you need to talk about your love life, I'm here."

She snorts softly. "I might believe you if you didn't look like I was about to pull your teeth when you say that."

It's one of my faults, not being able to keep the truth off my face. "I'm only grimacing because I'm the last person you should ask for advice. Outside of Logan, my batting average is zero. I'm not sure how I landed him, but I sure am glad I am not in the dating arena anymore."

"We're not dating. We're not... Anything."

She says it with banality, so I don't pry further. I'll have better luck if I ask Sherlock anyway. He's less bristly and more forthright about things.

I remember to ask her about my so-called cousin and his claim of being Maria Grace's guardian angel. The skeptical expression she pulls mirrors my own wariness. "I'll see what I can find out," is all she says before she vanishes.

It's late, but Daddy messages me, asking if I'm awake. I call him. "Hey."

He's a night owl. "Can't sleep?"

"Too much on my mind." *And bladder.* "What's up?"

"Your basketball player has quite a temper. His background check was clean, but a bit too sanitized for my liking. I dug deeper and found that there had been three incidents. Two happened when he was a juvenile, so those records are sealed, but I have a department friend who remembered details because he was a fan—emphasis on was. My informant has to remain anonymous, so keep this close, but Drew beat up a teammate pretty bad after a high school game, and he purposely ran his car into a dilapidated barn on his family's property after a girlfriend broke up with him. As an adult, he had civil charges brought against him by a woman who claimed Drew threatened her because he believed she was stalking his mother. It never went to trial, because they settled out of court. Nothing was done about the barn incident, either, since his parents didn't care. He's always been a star athlete, and a lot of stuff was slid under the carpet to protect him."

"Thanks for the info."

"Are you in danger from him? Has he threatened you?"

"Not me. Kit knew his parents, and I think Drew has a vendetta against her."

"Has he done anything to warrant getting the police involved?"

Fortunately, or unfortunately, no. "Nothing I can prove yet."

"Do you know how long he's in town? Does Kit need protection? Should I put a bug in Landon's ear?"

Detective Jones is barely on speaking terms with me, and because it's not complete radio silence is only due to the fact he's been good friends with my dad for so long. They were once partners on the force. "As far as I know, Drew and his father are only here for the weekend. At this point, there's nothing to report, and I'd rather not alert Drew that we suspect him of anything."

"Okay, kiddo. You say the word, and I am all over him, you got that?"

"Love you, Daddy. You're the best."

After disconnecting, I rush to the bathroom and relieve my poor bladder. When I return, I discover my husband waiting for me. "What can I help with?"

He's talking about the ceremony and reception, hoping to put my stressful mind at ease. "I finished reviewing our list for tomorrow, and we're on track. There's nothing you need to worry about."

"Except you."

"No worrying about me either. I'm fine." Except for the fact my bladder already is insisting on a bathroom run again.

He gives me *that* look. The one that tells me he knows me too well to buy my statement. "I've cleared my schedule for tomorrow, so I can spend it with you. You take care of the details for our big day, and I'll take care of you."

What would I do without him? I smile and extend my arm across the desk. "Deal. I have to say it sounds like I'm getting the better end of this."

He grins and shakes my hand. "I can think of a few ways you can make it up to me on our honeymoon."

"You are dauntless."

"Do you need more tea?"

Goodness, no. "Not at the moment. I could use some help with research, though."

His eyes light with curiosity. Nothing a lawyer enjoys more than diving into facts and information. "For what?"

"I need to figure out what motivation Bobby V and his boss have for hanging around the barn. They are cognizant of me, they know I'm a medium, but they won't speak to me, and I can't get them to leave. There has to be a reason. As ghosts, they can participate in reliving those time loops, but why would they? Who would want to sit at a table and play poker forever? At least Grimes seems to be content to do that. Bobby seems rather bored, which is why he was tossing things at your mother, I think."

His brow wrinkles. "If he were alive, I'd take him to task."

"Yeah, it's tough to punch a ghost in the face, but there has to be other ways we can get rid of him. I need to see what I can dig up about their lives and their deaths. What could be anchoring them here, and where their bones are buried."

"I'll grab my laptop."

While he does that, I pee and join him on the couch with my own. I do a search on Bobby V, while he takes Grimes.

"Randall Grimes," Logan says, scanning a list of search engine results. "I'll start at the top and work my way down."

"We need to know how, when, and where he died."

As he scans through the entries, I become lost in all the facts, as well as some of the legends, revolving around Thornhollow's most famous gangster. Bobby V was a busy guy during his thirty-three years on this earth. I can't help but get off track, reading some of the personal stories I stumble across from a local historian, who has published his work online.

"Grimes served six years in a state penitentiary after he was arrested for making moonshine and transporting it across state lines." Logan scans his screen, scrolling as he reads. "This was after Prohibition had been repealed, but the country was still feeling the effects of The Depression. He claimed to have turned a new leaf and was going into legitimate business, raising goats." We exchange a look, and Logan shrugs. "He returned to the land he had previously owned, found some squatters on it, and ran them off. About six months later, the police believed one or more of them came back and killed him in his sleep."

"He lived across the county line?"

Logan nods. "Does that help?"

"Not really. I thought maybe he'd died closer to the winery, so there has to be another anchor keeping him there."

"Could it be Bobby?"

I mimic Winter's earlier comment. "Anything is possible."

"Where did he die?"

I scroll through the historian's facts about Bobby's last days. "There's a problem with that. The official record states he ran from Thornhollow and was never seen again. Others claim he was killed in a shootout with Grimes. There's yet another eyewitness account that states he left and came back, secretly living in the old orphanage where he grew up. It had been abandoned by that point. There was a body found there that seemed to match his description, but it was badly decomposed. The coroner's report was inconclusive as to who it was. The body was then relocated to the pauper cemetery outside of town."

We continue our separate research, exchanging a few details around the timelines each man lived, but eventually growing weary of the hunt. It's after midnight when we call it quits and return to bed.

I miss the sunrise, dozing around my bathroom runs, but not getting any deep sleep. I tread downstairs, grateful I have no clients to worry about today, except myself, and allow

Logan to serve me coffee and breakfast. I am reluctant to eat, but too tired to argue with him and devour the pancakes he puts in front of me.

Gloria arrives before eight with her mobile sewing kit, a rolling suitcase filled with supplies, an iron, and extra fabric left from my gown. A slight woman, it's amazing she can handle all of it on her own. She whisks me upstairs to look at the dress.

"This is all wrong," she says, shaking her head as I stand there, having lost several pounds of water, and yet, still only able to get the zipper halfway up the side. I feel a bit woozy and place a hand on the wall to steady myself. "You are too pale, *cherie*. What have you been doing to yourself these past few days?"

"Sage gave me a tea to slim down. What do you think? Is there any hope you can fix this?"

She makes a twirling motion and I pivot in a slow circle. The vertigo worsens and I nearly stumble, saved by her grabbing my wrist. "No more tea," she pronounces. "You're harming yourself."

Tears suddenly fill my eyes and I brush at a few that spill from the corners. "Everything is a mess."

"Nonsense." She surveys my backside. A soft sound escapes her lips, as if she's having an *aha* moment and she mutters something in French.

"What?" I crane my head too fast to try and see behind me and nearly end up toppling both of us to the floor.

"The insert."

"What about it?"

Propping me against the dresser, she unzips the dress. "Take this off and go sit before you pass out."

I do as instructed, letting her capable hands help. "What's up with the insert? It looks fine to me."

Laying the voluminous material over her arm, she shakes her head and wags a finger. "Do not worry. I will have this fixed in no time."

"You will?" The insert is a small band—I can't believe it has anything to do with my problem. "How?"

At the door, she leans out and calls down the stairs for Logan to bring up her suitcase. Then she whirls on me. "You doubt me?"

No, but I sense she's reluctant to tell the truth and that worries me. "You're taking it out?"

"We will find a suitable solution."

"There isn't another spot for it without messing up the composition and form." My voice comes out sharper and more panicky than I mean it to.

She sits next to me on the mattress, showing me the lovely band of lace and satin that holds great meaning to me. "When Joseph sewed this in, it caused the material at the waist to constrict here and here." She runs a finger over the edges on each side. "The band is too wide. I must remove it."

"Wait, so you're saying I didn't gain weight?"

"Not a pound." She winks. Then her astute gaze sizes me up. "You always look like you could use more, not less."

"But how are you going to fix it?"

She pats my hand, and we hear the clunk of her rolling suitcase outside the door. "Have faith, *ma cherie*."

"We can't let Logan see the dress," I hiss.

"Thank you," she calls to him. "You may leave it there."

"Everything okay?"

"*Oui*. Now go away."

His footsteps head downstairs.

Gloria smiles at me. "Perhaps you should lie down and rest."

Actually, I feel like I can breathe again. My head feels clearer than it has in days, but my body betrays my insistence that I'm fine when I yawn widely. I hate to take time to nap, but I'm exhausted.

My balance is still off, but I manage to make it to my bed. Before I can set my phone app for fifteen minutes, I hear Aunt Willa's sewing machine going, Gloria humming away. As I close my eyes, a smile creeps over my face. I have no idea how she's going to do it, and although I want to hover over her shoulder and watch, I let it go. My dress could not be in better hands.

TWENTY-ONE

The alarm goes off, and I shoot up. Although it feels like I just closed my eyes, a glance at the time tells me, that, no, in fact, it has been the allotted fifteen minutes. There's a cup of freshly brewed coffee and a muffin on the nightstand. I assume these are complements of my husband, or maybe Kit.

As I gobble down the food, alternating bites of the delicious lemon and raspberry treat that can only be from The Bee Hive with sips of coffee, I relish both. I am *so* done with licorice-flavored tea.

I head to the main floor, light on my feet and ready to tackle the day anew.

There's an unexpected convention in my living room. Logan, Mama, Brax, Kit, Lia, and Sage are gathered. "Rosie and Jenn are at the church," Mama says. She's using her authoritative, take-no-prisoners tone. Scanning the yellow notepad from my desk, she talks me through the items. "I spoke to Betty and all the flowers are in order and ready. She will be there before rehearsal this afternoon with the plants you ordered to decorate the pulpit and surrounding area. She's also bringing extra ribbon in case we need it. Brax will do a trial run with your hair and makeup, and we've decided you should wear it up with ringlets along your face."

I bark a laugh. "What? Who's *we*?" I glance at my best friend. "I'm going with it down in waves. We've already discussed this."

Brax towers over all of us, but right now he looks like a five-year-old who's in trouble. His dark eyes flick to my mother, then back to me with a pleading expression. "I told Dixie I would entertain the idea and discuss it with you. We can try both styles and see which you prefer."

"I already know what I prefer."

Mama raises her nose. "Your face is just like mine and Willa's, and you'll look prettier with it up."

I pinch my lips together. "Mama, this is *my* wedding, and I happen to like my hair down."

The corners of her eyes narrow, emphasizing her crow's feet. "Remember the prom? The one you went to with that Cassian boy?"

Lia lights up. "Ooh, was he cute?"

My hair had been long and it ended up caught in the back zipper of my dress, causing me to miss half the dinner at the Country Club because Mama and I couldn't get the mess untangled. We broke the zipper and had to cut a chunk of my strands off.

Brax snorts, obviously recalling the embarrassing night.

Logan glances about, confused. "What happened?"

I point a finger at Brax. "Not a word." I turn it on Mama. "You either. Trust me, there will be no hair incidents tomorrow."

She gives me a look that says *we'll see about that*, then

continues reading off the list with her updates. When she's finished, she regards me. "Everything is under control. There's nothing else you need to do until the rehearsal at three. If anything comes up, you call me, understand?"

She's used to taking charge but isn't especially good at organizing events. Typically, she turns that over to other people. I wonder why she's stepped in today to manage what's left before the big event. "Is there a reason you're doing this?"

She lowers the tablet and purses her lips. "I know what's going on." Her voice is quieter than normal and has an edge to it. She hates that I'm a medium, but also respects that I do it. "You have other things to attend to, and we're all concerned you're trying to juggle too much."

Logan doesn't meet my eyes, and I suspect they're in cahoots. Kit steps next to me, shoulder to shoulder. "You're amazing, Miss Dixie. I promise we'll take good care of her."

A brusque nod from Mama tells me the conversation is over. She turns to Sage. "I sure could use some tea."

Sage, who has failed to hide a grin, flashes her a big smile. "Come to the shop. I have a new chai blend that I think you'll love."

Mama hugs me and walks out. Sage lowers her voice, as we watch her go. "Do you want to try the séance this afternoon?"

Lia bobs up and down on the balls of her feet. "I do!"

This is one of those moments when I wish I could give my gift to her. She would love it, and do a lot of good with it, rescuing earthbound ghosts and making them famous in the process. "I thought you had school until two."

"We always get out early for the parade on Thursday and don't go back until Monday."

News to me. I shake my head at Sage. "You're too busy." Even now, I see the street and parking lot are packed with cars. All her outside tables are filled and there's a line out the door. "Get back to Raven. We'll meet tonight after the rehearsal dinner. Does that work for you both?"

"We'll be there. How's the dress?"

The sewing machine upstairs is running like a hamster on a wheel. Over it, Gloria continues humming. I wonder if she knows how much both sounds ease my worries. "Everything is under control."

"No more tea?"

I stick out my tongue. "No offense, but I'm never drinking that stuff again. I will say, it did the trick. I was peeing all night."

"Be sure you drink plenty to rehydrate."

She leaves and I nudge Lia to go with her. "Nope," my young friend says, kicking off her Keds and dropping into Rosie's desk chair. "Raven says I chat too much with the customers, slowing down the line. She told me to help you today."

"You? Talk too much?" I layer my voice with incredulousness. "I can't believe it."

She throws a pen at me like a dart, and I deflect it, both of us laughing. It feels good to be able to joke. "I'm definitely bringing my equipment to the séance tonight."

I start to argue, then decide against it. The girl has a mind of her own. "As long as it's okay with your mom."

She works the mouse of Rosie's computer and starts typing. "I'm going with Wedding Bells and Happy Tales for the blog. I'm still toying with names for the podcast. Branding is important and I want to keep it consistent, but I don't like to be tied into only one thing. I can still use Tales—

Tales from The Chapel." She pauses, cocking her head to one side. "I like it!"

"You're not interviewing me for a podcast."

She grins. "No worries."

I know that grin. "Lia," I say in warning. "What are you up to?"

She gives me an innocent, wide-eyed expression. "What would I be up to?"

Logan motions Kit and Brax to the kitchen, while I give her an evil eye. "You run everything by me before it's published—blog posts *and* podcast episodes."

She snaps off a mock salute. "You're the boss."

There's a level of snark in her tone that makes me edgy, but I leave her be.

"Sorry about the hair thing," Brax says when I join the others. "You know how your mother is."

I've already let that go and am wondering if there are any more muffins. "I know. She's not Helen, but she does like to get her way."

"Tell me about it." He turns to Kit. "Any chance you'll do readings this afternoon?"

"I really should stay here," she says. "If everything goes right, I'll be back in the saddle next week."

He gives her a pat on the back, drops a kiss on my head, and exits through the back door.

"You look as if you're feeling better," Kit says to me.

"I am, and we're going to resolve the ghost stuff tonight. Hopefully, your problem, too."

Logan leans back on the counter, crossing his legs at his ankles. "If you two are okay, I'm going to visit Mother and see if I can get Winston alone long enough to question him about Brianna."

"Oh, I'm coming for that," Kit says.

It's one more piece of the puzzle we need solved, but I fear it could open a can of worms we don't want at the moment.

Gloria calls down. "Ava, it's ready."

"Hold that thought," I tell them. "Don't do anything yet."

I hustle upstairs and find Gloria frowning at the dress where it lies on the bed. "Oh, no, it didn't work?"

Her furrowed brow clears and she smiles at me. "We won't know until we try."

She orders me into the gown, and I notice the band of special fabric is still in the deep V of the back. "I thought you were going to take it out." I slip the gown on and she adjusts the shoulders.

"I had a better idea."

She forces me to lift my left arm, and what do you know, the zipper goes all the way up. The material is snug around my curves, but not too tight. I laugh, practically giddy. "It worked."

Gently turning me so I can see the backside in the mirror, she sticks her finger between my spine and the material, pulling it out and letting it snap back. "Magic," she says with a grin.

"You added elastic?"

"You're hardly the first bride to have issues with the fit of her dress right before her ceremony. Do you think I don't have a few tricks up my sleeve?"

I lift my arms and shimmy my hips. The satin and lace shifts with me. "You are amazing." I wrap my arms around her and give her a fierce squeeze. "I can't thank you enough."

I'm changing back into my street clothes when Winter

calls. Gloria is packing up her supplies, and I put the phone between my shoulder and ear so I can help. "Tabitha isn't far off the mark," Winter tells me. "It's possible you could enter the in-between and come out somewhere else, but it's unlikely unless you move around, such as chasing a ghost while you're in there. Think of it as trains on multiple tracks. Each time-space fractal is a car on one track. If you stay in yours, you'll return at the same starting point. If you hop into a different train's car, you'll end up somewhere else, or maybe some *time* else."

"So, I shouldn't move if I end up in the in-between?"

"Correct."

"But I can slip in, talk to the ghost, and come back out without issue."

"In theory. I'm not versed in quantum physics. We know parallel universes and alternate dimensions exist, but entering one of them, regardless if you stay put once you're there, is risky. I've been in an alternate reality and it was... bad. The best way to deal with your stuck ghost is to call her to you in a controlled environment like Persephone suggested."

She'd never shared the details of the time she'd ended up stuck in the ghost realms, but I knew what had happened. Luckily, both she and her fiancé had survived. "We're holding a séance tonight." Gloria zips her bag and eyes me. She knows of my talents and is sometimes curious about them. "That's the best container I've got, and if I get Maria Grace and Nettie together, I can cross them at the same time. That should bring their lingering souls peace."

"Be careful. I know you're getting to be an old hand at this, but the in-between is nothing to mess with."

"I have no intention of visiting it from here on out." All I needed to do was get Maria Grace out of it. "I've got my tools and Sage, and the others will be there."

"How's Kit?"

I walk Gloria into the hall. She bumps her wheels over the edge of the carpet runner, following me. I hold up a finger to make her wait. "Hold on," I say to Winter and call down to Logan. He emerges and sees what I need, bounding up to grab the suitcase. I speak to Winter once more. "She's handling it better than I would."

Logan leads the two of us downstairs, easily carrying the luggage. In the background, I hear one of Winter's sisters calling for her to handle the cash register. "Sorry, I've got to run," she says, begrudgingly. "Let me know how the séance goes."

We disconnect and I walk Gloria to her car, thanking her again for saving the day. She tells me she'll see me at the ceremony and waves as she drives off.

I find Kit sitting next to Lia, both hunched over Rosie's screen. They glance up in unison and then right back to the keyboard, avoiding my eyes.

"What are you two up to?"

Lia turns the screen away when I try to peek. "Nothing."

Kit straightens and blocks my view. "Did you get the dress fixed?"

"Don't change the subject."

She takes my arm and leads me to my office, lowering her voice. "The kid's working on something for you. A gift. I promise it's not about ghosts or anything to do with blogs and podcasts."

I couldn't fathom what that might be. "Fine. Now, about confronting Winston. Can it wait until Sunday? Please?"

"You want me to sleep with this thing"—she points to the crown—"two more nights?"

"Maybe Sage can draw sigils on you again. It's just that if we confront him today, he might quit or bug out before I get Maria Grace and her mother crossed over, and also there's the reception. If he quits before that, St. Helen will stroke out."

Her disappointed sigh is so loud, it's Oscar-worthy and makes me feel like a heel. "Fine. I suppose I can wait."

"Thank you."

The doorbell rings and we discover Doc outside. He holds up a brown envelope. "A colleague put a rush on your test results. Thought you might want to know what they found."

Kit's face pales.

I grip her hand. "Come on in. Can I get you something? Water? Coffee?"

"No need. This won't take long."

Her fingers tighten on mine. "I think I might be the one who needs a drink," she murmurs.

TWENTY-TWO

Logan emerges from the kitchen and helps Doc remove his coat. "You can use my office if you want."

"Up to you," Doc says to Kit.

Her hand practically crushes mine, hanging on for dear life. Behind us, Lia stops typing. "Here's fine. Go ahead," she says, putting on a brave face even though her aura, which has caught my attention, has gone bleak.

"All right." He glances at my desk. "May I?"

I wave him into my space. "Of course."

He retrieves several papers and photos, laying them on the surface side by side. Grabbing a pen, he uses the tip to point at the first series of black-and-white pictures. "This is your brain. See these areas here?"

We all lean forward. Lia rushes in and grabs Kit's other hand.

Kit swallows. "What about them?"

"The architecture of your brain suggests high intelligence, but also something else that many of my colleagues have dismissed their whole careers and will continue to do so, even in the face of scientific evidence. These areas"—he points to other places of gray matter right under the top of her head—"are larger than average, and I'm postulating the flow of information is greater and more efficient. This pattern suggests cognitive strengths in problem solving and sensory integration."

"Whoa," Lia says. "You can tell all that from that mess?"

"Okay...?" Kit swallows hard. "What are you getting at? There's no tumor, right? No growth or aneurysm?"

He chuckles and hands her two sheets of medical jargon typed under the hospital's logo. "Your brain appears to be as healthy as young Lia here. I'd love to know your secret."

Her shoulders slump in relief and her white knuckle grip on me loosens. Lia jumps up and down, yelling, "Hooray!" and Logan pats Kit on the back.

"I..." She shakes her head and chuckles, scanning the report. "I don't know what to say."

He sets down the pen and smiles at her. "I expect you to report for duty Monday."

"Monday?"

"The clinic opens at nine. If you don't have any conflicts with that time, bring coffee. The stuff there is disgusting. And if you're willing, there's a cognitive study I'd like to enroll you in. You've completed the initial tests, and I'm on the medical research team, so I can share information about the study once you join. It doesn't pay much, but we're on the cutting edge of discoveries with mapping the brain and understanding what makes each unique. I'd love you to be part of it."

He leaves us all smiling and congratulating her. Logan

hands Lia several bills. "Run across the street and get some celebratory cupcakes, will you?"

She snatches the money. "Told you," she calls over her shoulder as she races out. "I knew you were special, Kit."

The next few hours whiz by, and Brax returns to do my hair and makeup. Raven and Sage ask Lia to work their register, regardless of her penchant to talk.

Upstairs in front of the mirror, Brax coaxes me to try an idea with my hair. I reluctantly agree. An hour later, I'm glad I did. After using a special curling iron to make beachy waves, he's swept one side up with a sparkling white comb, allowing a few strands to frame my face. The other is down, the ends brushing my shoulders. He insists I wear the same jewelry as I will tomorrow, and he even applies false lashes before finishing the rest. When he finally turns me around in the chair so I face the mirror, I can't believe it's me.

"How did you do that?" I turn my head side to side, my diamond earrings catching the lights and sparkling like the comb. My eyes look bigger, my cheeks defined, and my lips fuller. "You do have a gift, you know."

He chuckles. "You don't grow up with Queenie and not learn a few tricks about beauty and using every available tool in your arsenal to knock people off their feet."

"I remember when we used to get into that huge drawer she had in the center of her mirrored dresser. What were we, five? Six?"

"I'm grateful she never questioned my love of girlie things. I never particularly wanted to wear this stuff myself, but I sure enjoyed helping with her face and hair. Always felt as if it was an art to me, kind of like painting her nails."

Which makes me look at my own. Eep. I hold them up. "Will you have time to do these tomorrow?"

"Don't worry." He pats my shoulder. "Rhys is the guy you want for that."

I admire my hair in the reflection once again, toying with a tendril. "Color me surprised. I love this look," I confide.

"The best of both worlds." He adjusts the comb. "You're going to knock 'em dead."

Our eyes meet in the mirror, and we cringe, then laugh. "I don't need more ghosts on my hands," I say. "I'm already afraid the ones at the reception might cause problems."

"No luck getting them to move on to the afterlife?" At the shake of my head, he rolls his eyes. "Why would any of them not want to do that? Why hang around in a smelly old barn?"

Thankfully, it's not smelly at the moment. "There are plenty of reasons. The two that concern me the most lived a pretty rough life. They might fear what's waiting for them on the other side."

"Ah." He gathers combs, brushes, and the curling iron. "If there's anything I can do...?"

Since before elementary school, he's been defending me, protecting me, but also letting me fight my own battles when I wanted to. I pinch his beefy bicep. "If only you could toss them out of the barn permanently."

"Sounds like you need a spirit bouncer."

I rise, anticipating the look on Logan's face when he sees me. "You're right. I do. If you hear of any, let me know."

I feel like a true bride, even though I'm not walking down the aisle but rather my stairs to find everyone waiting for me. Mama, Daddy, Kit, and, of course, Logan. There are several extras, as well. Persephone and Sherlock. Tabitha and Samuel.

A delighted hush falls as they spy me. I stop at the

bottom and lift my arms, twirling. "Well? What do you think?"

Their eyes are wide, their lips curved in smiles. Mama's hand goes to her heart, and Daddy says, "Absolutely stunning."

Tabitha and Samuel nod, and I see Sherlock slip his hand into Persephone's. She doesn't pull away. Lia rushes from the kitchen, and pulls up short, her mouth falling open. "Wow."

Logan steps toward me. "Wow is right. You're breathtaking."

My cheeks heat, and I raise my gaze to his as he takes my hands. "What about the hair?"

His attention doesn't leave my face. "It's perfect."

Mama clears her throat. "Just imagine how good you would look with both sides up."

Kit groans, and Daddy chuckles. Moxley barks.

"Take what you can get, Mama," I warn.

She makes a huffing noise, but there's no real irritation in it. "It's your wedding, Ava. Like Logan said, it's perfect."

Together, we walk as a group to the church, including Mox who will be part of the ceremony. The air is crisp but the sun is warm.

I've put the dog's tiny bow tie on his collar and he struts beside us as if he realizes his importance. The only one who doesn't come inside is Kit. "I'm feeling pretty good," she tells me outside the rear entrance. Betty's van is parked close by. "I want to make up for putting Brax and Rhys in a bind. It's Friday night, the festival is underway, and I can do some ten-minute speed readings."

Brax overhears her as he joins us. "Are you sure? Don't feel obligated."

She taps the crown. "This will protect me, and if anything does start to bother me, I'll quit and call Sage to come to ink me up."

I rub her arm. "Don't overdo it, and if anybody suspicious shows up, you text me right away and get out of there, okay?" She doesn't have her car, so I explain where my keys are. "And be sure you come back here to sleep tonight. It's not safe for you at your house yet."

She gives me a gentle embrace. "I can't thank you enough for all you've done for me, especially right now when you're so swamped. I'll check in after a while, and I'll be available for the"—she stops and lowers her voice—"after-party, if you get my meaning."

The séance. I'm having second thoughts about trying it tonight. Everything is going so well and upsetting Helen isn't the best idea. "I'll let you know if it's still on."

Brax offers to walk her to my place, but she waves him off. "We really appreciate this," he says to her. "There will be a line out the door as soon as everyone hears you're back."

We watch her jog across the parking lot and disappear down the alley.

Helen appears at the door, body tense as she scans me from head to toe. "You're late. Reverend Stout is waiting."

Logan steps to her side, putting a comforting hand on her. "You look lovely tonight, Mother."

Instantly, she relaxes and smiles up at him. "It's finally happening. I've been planning this weekend since you were three."

I have the feeling it was even before that. He turns her around, leading her inside and winking at me over his shoulder.

TWENTY-THREE

Two hours later, we're all practiced out.

Daddy and I have walked down the aisle, Logan and I pretended to recite our vows, and our attendants have run through what they'll do with the bouquet and rings. Mox is exhausted.

Arriving at the Country Club for dinner, we find the place packed. This may be normal for a Friday night—I don't visit enough to know. Logan and his family are founding members, and for them, it's a second home.

Or the crowd could be due to the numerous tourists in town for the festival, and many in the community are flocking here to avoid the other establishments.

The hostess manning the entrance greets Helen and LC, Logan's father, with a smile and congratulations on tomorrow's ceremony. Her eyes light up when she spots Logan, and I try not to take offense when she barely glances at me. She hands us off to a staff member in the customary black suit with the Club's gold emblem and he escorts us past the large common area to a private room inside the restaurant with a small bar and personal servers. They've pushed two banquet tables together to accommodate our group, and have covered them in white cloths with arrangements to match our bridal colors.

Thankful I can eat but still cautious about fitting easily into my dress, I order my favorite sandwich. Helen seems perplexed, and a bit disgruntled, that regardless of everyone else indulging in the most expensive plates, I'm easily satisfied with a simple item.

Aside from that, the meal goes well, our families, friends, and the reverend and his wife keeping things lighthearted and fun. I say a silent prayer that tomorrow goes this smoothly.

I have to ignore a few ghosts along the way, but it's not them that sour the night for me. As we're leaving, I spot the dean. Howard waves from across the crowded space, and I tug at Logan's arm. "Time to go."

My retreat is thwarted by Helen. "Dean Hurley," she calls, seemingly delighted. "I didn't know you were in town."

Logan and I exchange a look. His mom will surely find out that Howard has offered Logan the temporary teaching position, but maybe since she's focused on him taking over her legacy, she won't care that he's turned it down.

Howard cuts through the tables, nodding jovially at folks as he goes. I hold in a long-suffering sigh, Logan squeezes my hand and says to Helen, "Dr. Hurley and Drew are visiting for the festival."

The dean is in high spirits, lifting a glass of dark liquid to us. "Good to see you, Helen. LC." The rest of our party has excused themselves and headed for the exit. "I'm here with Landon."

He motions over his shoulder and it's only then that I

spot Detective Jones next to the seat Howard vacated. His dark eyes narrow when he meets my gaze. Since when does he belong to the Country Club? More importantly, did Daddy say something to him about Drew? Could that be why he's here? If there's one thing I've learned about Jones, he's a wily one. He always has something up his sleeve.

I consider confronting him but a touch of anxiety hums under my skin. "Where is your son, Dr. Hurley?"

Howard sways, suggesting he's had more than a few shots of his chosen beverage. "Drew is out with friends. They were going to the coffee bar and said something about that place across the street." He frowns and makes a circling gesture with his finger. "What's the name of it? The Croaky Toad?"

A chill shoots down my spine. "That doesn't seem like Drew's kind of scene."

There's a ringing in my ears, and I pardon myself, not waiting for his reply. I stop next to a statue of a rider on a horse, looking to play polo, and pull out my phone. Kit's rings three times and goes to voicemail. I almost stomp my foot in frustration.

The noise of the packed crowd is loud enough that I plug my other ear, speaking over it but turning my back so those nearby don't hear what I have to say. "I know you're busy, but heads up, Drew is visiting The Toad tonight. I think it would be in your best interest to get out of there. Call, or text me, and let me know you're okay."

Both Brax and Logan are staring at me when I end the call. I point at the exit and mouth, *I'm going outside. Need some air.*

I make it to the parking lot when they catch up to me at

Logan's car. "Get in," Logan says, opening the passenger door.

It's nice not to have to explain my panic. "Thank you." Mama is messaging me about the abrupt departure. "I'm sure Kit is fine." Am I trying to convince myself, or them? "But she's not answering and I need to know for certain."

"She's probably with a client," Brax says. He reaches from the backseat to pat my shoulder. "Plus, Rhys is there, and she's surrounded by people."

Before we hit the road to downtown, my phone rings. I start to ignore it, thinking it's Mama, but it's Kit. "He's not here," she says without preamble. "It's all good."

I drop my head against the seat and let go of a relieved sigh. "Thank goodness. Still, he could be on his way. He's with friends." At this time of night, more liquor is being served than coffee. "I'd feel better if you came home."

"You worry a lot, don't you?"

"You have no idea."

Her voice is light, teasing. "Since when is The Wedding Chapel my home?" At my silence, she chuckles. "Do not cut your evening short because of me. I'm heading out right now. I'll see you later."

I relate what she said to Logan and Brax. Logan's cell goes off. Mine does as well, but I'll call her back. His built-in Bluetooth brings up *St. Helen*.

"Aw, you changed her 'Mother' moniker to my nickname for her."

He shoots me a grin. "True love knows no bounds." He taps a button on the screen, using the speaker to talk to her. "Sorry for the abrupt exit, but Ava isn't feeling so good."

She blows right over that. "Everyone is coming to the

estate for a nightcap. You should, too. We need to run through tomorrow's itinerary one more time."

He starts to beg off but then glances at me with a question in his eyes. This could be our way into the house to pull off the séance. I nod and announce, "I'm feeling better. Just needed fresh air. If we're going to review the schedule, I'd like to invite a few others to join us."

Her pause is brief, but she acquiesces. "Fine. See you shortly."

Once he's disconnected, I call Mama. "Hey, Mama. Are you going to the Cross estate?"

"No. Why? Are you okay? You looked upset when you left."

I have a sinking feeling that the majority of our wedding party is not. Were they even invited? Landon isn't the only one with something up his sleeve tonight. No doubt, Helen wants to discuss the future of the winery with Logan. I wonder why she's allowing me to crash her plans by bringing my friends. "You were invited, though, right?" I'm ready to take Helen to task.

"Yes, of course, but I've had enough of you-know-who for one day."

I make a sorry face at Logan but he waves it off. I text Sage to alert her to our plan.

"It's been a long day for all of us. I'll see you and Daddy first thing tomorrow."

"Love you, sweetheart," Daddy calls into the phone.

"Love you both." I disconnect and continue conversing with Sage. She's bringing Raven. That makes three for our circle, and I'm sure Persephone will be there, but I need two more physical entities. Logan will have to keep his mother and father occupied and out of our hair. I don't want to endanger Kit. I twist in my seat to look at Brax. "Would you be up for a séance?"

His face pales. "I didn't realize being your man-of-honor would require talking to ghosts."

"It doesn't, but being my friend does." I wink. "I know you need to get to The Toad, so if you can't go with us, I understand."

He claps his hands together and rubs them, a grin spreading across his face. "Don't be silly. I'm glad to help. And just so you know, Rhys will be so jealous."

"I could use him, as well, if he could get away for an hour."

He shifts forward to remove his phone from his back pocket. "He's terrified of ghosts, but I'm sure he wouldn't miss this for the world."

"What about Lia?" Logan asks. "You promised she could come."

"Technically, I didn't promise, and since we don't know exactly how powerful this psychic witch is, I'd rather be on the safe side and keep her out of it."

"Good call." We head for his parents'. "I assume you're keeping me out of it as well?"

I can't tell if he's relieved or disappointed. "I need you to run interference with your mom. Keep her occupied. This could take five minutes or twenty. You might also have to keep Winston distracted. If he's Brianna's channel, he might sense something is up, or she could warn him and blow my plans to get Nettie and Maria Grace together."

He nods, and after Brax hangs up with Rhys, we fall quiet, each of us lost in our own thoughts. I'm not sure which entity I'm more worried about ruining my plans—Brianna or my mother-in-law.

TWENTY-FOUR

Making small talk with LC and Helen in the study only increases my anxiety about what is yet to come. I'm waiting for Sage and Raven to show, along with Rhys. I've explained that the three of them are going to help me with miscellaneous items tomorrow, acting as my backup for any potential problems that may arise. Helen seems to think this is a good idea but has to get in a zinger anyway. "You just thought of this tonight?"

Breathe, I remind myself. Whatever gets my friends in the door is worth it. "While I'm experienced with handling large parties, I won't be available to see to last-minute glitches or changes in plans. It seems wise to have several options in place."

Chuck is there, taking some of the spotlight off Logan. I sit back with Brax and act like I'm listening to the family chat, as Winston makes sure everyone is taken care of before he excuses himself for the night. Helen barely acknowledges him. "Remember, you're to be here an hour early."

"Yes, of course." He turns to me with a smile. "Don't

hesitate to contact me if you think of anything you need me to do prior to the reception."

His aura is a soft yellow and pink, suggesting he truly wants to be of service. I can't hide my relief that he's leaving, and won't be here to interfere with the séance. "Thank you. I'll be in touch."

He gives me a nod. "I hope to see your friend there." Then he leaves.

I just bet you do.

The others discuss the successful growing season, the latest investors who've come on board, and a few big meetings that'll be held over the winter. Nothing is said about tomorrow's schedule.

Helen is in her element, the queen in her palace, consulting with her advisors and ready to expand her empire. While they brainstorm ways to expand the north quarter of the vineyard, I mentally go over what I'll need to get Nettie and her daughter together and move them on. Luckily, before I'm ready to poke my eyes out, the doorbell rings. I jump up. "I'll get it. That'll be Sage and Raven."

Brax is more than happy to go with me, not even offering an excuse. As we scoot down the hallway, he shakes his head. "And I thought my mother was an enterprising mogul."

"The apple didn't fall far from the CEO tree," I tease. We meander through the maze of halls to the front entrance. "You're one to talk, with three businesses going."

"If I don't do it, Thornhollow won't have any of those places. We're lucky to have as many shops as we do, considering the size of our town."

He's right, of course. I know my mother and the City Council are always balancing bringing in industry and attracting tourism while keeping our safe neighborhoods and healthy employment stats. Capitalizing on our town's strengths, while not simply throwing it to the wolves, is a high-wire act. "I'm appreciative of the fact you and Queenie are so good at your jobs." I open the door to see the sisters. Both are carrying large satchels filled with the tools we need. "Sage, too."

She lifts a brow. "Me, too, what?"

I grab her arm and draw her across the threshold, Raven following. "I'm hooked on your raspberry tea, and I can't live without your muffins and cupcakes. Between you and Queenie, my life is filled with good food and equally good friends."

Rhys shows up before I close the door. He has Kit with him. "What's this?" I ask. "I thought you were going back to The Chapel."

"And miss the séance? No way. I'm helping with your pregnant ghost, but the rest is about me." She taps her chest with her thumb. "Again, you're being overly protective and worried about everybody but yourself. You have some unique gifts, Ava, but I'm the strongest psychic here. You wouldn't take on Brianna without the witches"—she points at Sage and Raven—"and you're not doing it without me, either."

I'm outnumbered, and I have to admit, her reasoning is solid. Maria Grace and her mother are one thing—to handle somebody of Brianna's level, even if she's a spirit, is another. I need all the help I can get. "Your admirer has already left for the day, so at least he won't be a problem."

She gives me a disgusted look. "Good. I'll deal with him another time."

I take them to the study so they can say hello before I tell Helen, "I'm going to give my team the tour and go through the schedule for tomorrow so they're familiar with the house and grounds. We'll catch up with all of you in a while."

My mother-in-law regards me, the sisters, and Kit. I see the wheels turning in her head.

We're not fooling her one bit. The only thing she's got wrong is that she thinks I'm going to exorcise the barn of the meddling ghosts there. Maybe, after we've crossed Nettie and Maria Grace, and possibly figured out how to get rid of Brianna, I'll take my posse and clean the speakeasy, as well.

That thought lifts my mood. I lead my co-conspirators to the small room off the kitchen, excited to get on with this. It's nearly impossible to get all of us inside the cramped space. Sage and Raven immediately go to work, using the items from Nettie's shelf, along with their tools to create a small chalk circle on the floor. Brax and Rhys stay clear by sitting on the thin mattress.

"Persephone. Sherlock," I call quietly. "We're ready."

"Ready for what?" a voice asks at my shoulder, startling me. "Oh, no. What have you done?"

"Hello, Nettie." I turn to see her lips peeled back, shock that her shrine to Maria Grace has been disturbed twisting her features. "It's time for your daughter to come home."

TWENTY-FIVE

N o one can see her but me, Kit, and Sage, though Brax and Rhys are both tense. Nettie cries and swoops at me. "Don't you touch her stuff! That's mine!"

I brace as she goes right through me, her phantom form as frigid as icicles scraping over my bones. I shudder, teeth chattering. "We need...the items...to call...her spirit."

Flying about, she shrieks. "Where is she then? Why isn't she here?"

Sage motions to the men to join us at the circle, forming an outer human barrier. She lights the candle in the center and begins chanting under her breath. Raven signals us to hold hands. Rhys is on my right, Kit on my left. He scans the tiny room frantically; she's tracking the spirit.

Where are Persephone and Sherlock? When Sage gives a nod, I have to go on without them. "Maria Grace, I call you to our circle. Come to us. Show yourself. Your mother is here. She's waiting for you."

Nothing happens.

Nettie wrings her hands in the corner. "Where is she?"

"What's happening?" Rhys whispers.

"Nothing, yet," I answer begrudgingly.

I call Maria Grace again and we wait. She doesn't come, and Nettie complains. Kit shoots me a look that suggests I should send her to the other side regardless.

I consider it. "Nettie, will you enter our circle, please?"

"Why?" Distrustful, she inches back, nearly fading into the wall.

The candle goes out. It seems to spur her back into anger. She screeches and lunges at me. "This isn't right. You're conjuring devils. Get out! Go away!"

I crouch to avoid her, releasing Rhys and Kit. Raven yells at me to not break the circle and Kit snaps at the ghost, "Stop that. We're here to help."

Nettie hits me full-on. The sensation is an ice-water bath. A sharp pain hits the back of my skull, and I gasp. When I open my eyes, reaching for Rhys and Kit's hands, they're not there. The room is white-washed, the ghostly dimension bare and cold.

Maria Grace seems to rise from the candlewick. There is no longer a flame. "Where am I?"

"At...the vineyard..." My teeth chatter. "Where your mother worked. Where you stole from the family to help your boyfriend."

She peers at all of my friends ghastly pale and unmoving, as if stuck in their own time. "Who are they?"

"They came to help," I tell her. "Your mother is here, too. Call her. Speak to her."

"Mama?"

I feel pressure against my skin, and then Nettie seems to push into our dimension. "Maria Grace? Is that you?" She gives a squeal of delight as she materializes in front of her daughter. The girl chokes on a sob, and the two embrace. "I can't believe you're here," Maria Grace says. "I was trying to come home, but..."

They both look at me. Unfortunately, we seem to be partially in the room, yet partially in the in-between. *Just don't move*, I tell myself. *Persephone*, I mentally call. *Help!*

With some relief, I see the lighted doorway spring up in my peripheral vision. I didn't consciously call it, but I'm not one to question a gift door to eternity. "Go to the light," I instruct. "It's time for you to be together again. You have a lot to catch up on."

Maria Grace rubs her belly. Nettie touches her baby bump and begins to cry. Neither looks confident about the lighted portal.

Persephone appears. "Ladies, if you'll follow us." Standing in the glow of the doorway is Maria Grace's guardian angel. He smiles at me, then her. "You're going to love it on the other side."

Between him and Persephone, the mother and daughter finally seem appeased. They clasp hands and talk all the way to the door. Before they walk into it, Nettie glances back at me. "I don't know who or what you are. I'm not even sure what happened here. But I thank you for bringing my daughter to me."

I lift a hand, feeling more like Reverend Stout than myself. "Go in peace. Be happy."

They disappear and the light winks out. Persephone and my ancestor stare at each other. "Well," he says, nervous. "Guess, I'm done here, too."

He starts to turn, and she stops him. "Actually, you have a new assignment."

"I do?"

She hands him a slip of paper that materializes out of nowhere. He reads it and glances at me. "I get to stay?"

My heart does a funny *thud* and I gawk at Persephone. "You're leaving me?"

She rolls her eyes. "I wish. He's here for Samuel."

My stomach falls. "To cross him?"

"Nope. He's received an extended stay because of you. All the good work you've done—with my help, of course—has earned you brownie points upstairs." She points toward heaven. "Also, Samuel is Tabitha's guide. However, since he's an earthbound spirit, he needs someone to keep him from getting into trouble. Gilbert, here, is his new guardian angel."

"Wait. Let me get this straight. Samuel is Tabitha's spirit guide, even though he's still a ghost."

She shrugs. "I don't make the rules. Now, we better get you to your correct time and place."

I feel a tug on my hand and suddenly everything snaps back to normal. My knees wobble and my throat is dry. Kit wraps an arm around my waist to steady me. "Good to see you looking alive again," she says. "There was a moment when I thought we lost you."

Wouldn't be the first time.

"Did it work?" Sage asks.

"It did." I allow Kit to help me to the bed and I plunk down. Rhys flutters to my side, asking if I need a drink. "Water would be good," I tell him.

Everyone wants to hear what happened, so I wait until he returns with a glass of ice water to give them details. I chug it, then use the back of my hand to wipe my lips. "And we have a new friend. A distant cousin of mine who is a guardian angel now for Samuel."

There's a surprised pause when everybody exchanges looks and then starts firing questions at me. I'm disappointed he and Tabitha aren't here to get the news first. Since I don't know much, and Persephone is nowhere to be seen, there aren't many I can answer.

I help Sage and Raven gather their tools and erase the circle. Once we're done, Brax wants to know, "What should we do with this?" He points to the items Nettie kept on her shelf.

"Do you know where Maria Grace is buried?" Raven lays them on the bed. "We could bury them with her."

"About that," I say, looking at Brax and Rhys. "Apparently, she's buried under the B&B."

Rhys' hand goes to his heart and he stumbles backward. "There's a dead woman under our house?"

Brax steadies him and we file from the room, me leading them outside and toward the barn. "At least her spirit won't bug you," I tell my friend, as I wind my arm through his. "She's enjoying life on the other side now."

Kit sidles up to me. "You didn't happen to get anything from Nettie about Brianna and Winston, did you?"

"I didn't want to stay in the ghost realm any longer than necessary. I'm sorry, I didn't ask."

She nods, but I see the consternation on her face. "We'll figure it out."

I feel bad. "Let's see what we can get out of the ghosts in the barn."

It's a good plan, but unfortunately, they aren't around. Both Kit and I reach out to them, but it's eerily quiet.

"This is weird," I say. "There's no one here, and not even the loops of time are playing."

Lia stumbles through the open doors, out of breath. "Did I miss it?"

"What are you doing here?" I ask.

She glowers, which, for her, is hard to pull off. "I got permission to come to the séance, and then you ghosted me."

"I wasn't sure how dangerous it might be. Sometimes when we pull spirits through into a séance, we get others we don't anticipate. I didn't want to take the chance that you might be in danger if Brianna showed up, rather than Maria Grace."

She balls her hands into fists, setting them on her hips. "I know that, and I was prepared. Stop treating me like a kid. I probably know more about earthbound spirits, and what they can do, than you do. You never even pick up a book, or watch any of the documentaries and scientific shows I recommend. This is what I want to do, and I'd give *anything* to be a ghost-whisperer like you. It's not fair that you're always trying to protect me and keep me away from them."

I step back, eyes wide. "No matter how much we prepare, things can get out of control quickly with spirits. I know you have far more book-learning about them than I do, but I have real-life experience."

"It's not your call. It's mine. I can't get experience if you don't let me attend these things. The best way to protect me is to let me be part of what you do, so I learn how to handle aggressive and violent spirits."

Since I was thrown into being a medium with no training, it's hard for me to argue with that. Still, I don't feel comfortable allowing an untrained minor to participate in most of what I do.

She continues. "I'm safer with you, no matter what's going on, than I am on my own, but I will do this either way."

It's Kit who comes to my rescue. "Why is this so important to you, Lia?"

She straightens, steel in her voice. "I want to be a voice for the dead. I know how much peace Ava brings to people, not only by communicating messages between the ghosts and those they left behind, but by assuring them there is an afterlife. I want to be involved with that."

Brax puts a hand on Lia's shoulder. "We're just trying to look out for you, kiddo."

Rhys smiles at her. "I don't understand why you want to hang out with ghosts, but I think Ava is right. Your safety comes first."

From the look on her face, I swear she's about to scream. "I'm not a kid! I can look out for myself."

"It wouldn't hurt her to observe," Sage says. "She doesn't have to participate in our circles or get directly involved in contacting spirits. For now, she can simply watch and use her equipment to get used to how they act."

Lia is nodding. "I'll do whatever you want."

It could still be dangerous, but it is an option. "I'll think about it, okay?"

"There are plenty of ways we can teach her how to protect herself when dealing with ghosts," Raven says. "We can strengthen her psychic abilities through lessons. I offer classes at Chicks With Gifts."

"I'm in," Lia says, pumping her arm.

I glance at Kit, and she nods. "Even with our abilities, it's good to train. Just like we can get stronger physically by working out, we can exercise our psychic muscles, and so can she. Everybody has them, why not use them?"

"Please, Ava," Lia begs. "Your passion is designing wedding gowns. Mine is helping spirits."

I feel myself caving. "As long as you take classes, and agree to do exactly what we say."

She hops up and down and claps. "Yes! I'll do it."

"We'll start your training next week," Sage says.

Lia looks like she's about to burst. "I can't wait."

We've been so wrapped up in this discussion, I don't hear the approaching footsteps until Dr. Hurley enters through the doorway. "Oh, there you are."

Kit freezes. So do I. "What are you doing here?" she demands.

"I came to see you." He steps inside, the overhead light casting a soft glow on his features. He looks tired, worn out. "I have a few things to say, and I need you to listen."

TWENTY-SIX

Everyone's attention snaps to Kit. She stands rigid. "There's nothing to say. You don't belong here."

The dean shakes his head. He appears more sober than earlier, but also less congenial. "I've been carrying around this stuff for years, and I need to get it off my chest. I drove by your place a dozen times in the last few days, trying to catch you. Attempting to talk to you." He holds out both hands to her, pleading. "Please. Hear me out."

Crossing her arms, she shakes her head. "There's nothing you can say that will change what happened, and it's not my job to relieve you of whatever guilt you're carrying. I saved your life."

Howard takes a step closer, and Brax and I shift so we're in front of Kit. "Maybe you didn't hear what the lady said." Brax glowers at the man, his voice low and dangerous. "She doesn't want to speak to you."

Howard's eyes stay on Kit, but he lowers his hands and doesn't move. "I'm sorry." He drops his eyes to the tops of his expensive loafers. His hands sink into his pockets. "All this time, I could have been with you and I was too stupid to realize how much you meant to me."

Again, we all glance at her. Does she want us to get rid of him? Does she want to hear him out? Her face is stony, and I can't tell, but her aura flares a blushing pink. Her arms stay crossed. "You *are* stupid."

He keeps his gaze averted. "It was impossible for me to wrap my head around what you told me. First of all, that my wife was trying to poison me, and then, the reason you knew that fact." He peeks at her through his lowered lashes. "I was an idiot, but it was just too much to take in. I don't even believe in that stuff..."

"I didn't need you to believe in *that stuff*. I needed you to believe in me."

He lifts his head slightly. "I know, I know. I wanted to. I did."

"Then why didn't you? We had something incredible."

He places a palm over his heart. "I've never felt about anyone the way I did you. The way I still feel about you."

The breath she sucks in is so quiet, so soft, I almost miss it. The pink spreads throughout her energy field. "Why now? Why did you hunt me down to tell me this?"

"Because I can't live with myself anymore. Not unless I apologize and beg you for forgiveness. Please, Kitty, take pity on me. I'm a silly old man who thought he knew everything. Thought his superior intelligence and powerful position at the college were all he needed in this world. I was wrong."

She swallows hard. Her folded arms fall to her sides. "You're telling the truth."

Something in her voice, or maybe the way she stares at him, spreads relief over his features. "And you know that because you're psychic."

She grunts a laugh. "No, you big dummy, I know that because I can see it in your face, hear it in your voice."

I press my lips together to keep from smiling. "Why don't we go to my place and talk about this some more? You can have privacy there."

"No," she says. "I want to hear more groveling."

Howard's head bobs. "I owe you that. I want you back in my life. I'll grovel from here to eternity if you will grant me that. Even if..." He sighs heavily. "Even if it's only as friends. And if you never want to see me again, I understand that, too, but I hope you'll still consider forgiving me for what I did."

Raven and Sage are grinning. Lia slides over to Kit's side and nudges her. "Come on, *Kitty*." At Kit's glare, she nudges her again. "It won't kill you to be his friend."

"Oh, I don't know. It might." Her glare turns on him. "I'm not sure I'm ready to forgive you, but I'll agree to hear you out."

At that moment, there's a commotion outside and the sound of running steps. "Dad!"

Drew. He bolts into the barn, pulling up short when he sees all of us.

At the same time, Helen calls from the house across the open ground, "What's going on out there?"

I meet Drew before he can come any farther, putting up my hands as stop signs. He overshadows me, but I stand my ground, feeling my best friend step behind me as backup. "You weren't invited, and you need to leave."

He frowns down at me. "I'm searching for my dad."

"And you found him, but this is a private conversation, and you can wait in your car."

He peers around Brax, pinning his father with a hard look. "Why are you talking to her?"

"That's my business." Howard lifts his chin. "Your mother and I didn't break up because of Kit. We broke up because Regina tried to kill me."

Drew takes a step back. "What are you talking about? Have you lost your mind?"

"You didn't tell him?" Kit asks.

"How could I?" Howard seems like his world is falling down around him. "It's one thing to find out that your spouse is trying to kill you, it's entirely another to explain such a thing to your child."

"You're making this up," Drew says. "Mother would never do something like that. You're looking for someone to blame for your failed marriage, and the person responsible is right there." He points at Kit.

"Your mother loves you," she says to him. "And so does your father. You're a very lucky man. But he's telling the truth. Yes, I fell in love with him, and yes, I wanted him to leave your mom. Not to hurt you, but to save himself. While your mother would do anything for you, that love became twisted. To try and keep your father, Regina poisoned him to make him sick. To make him need her more."

Howard steps toward Drew. "She's telling the truth. And yes, I believe she's psychic. I believe *in* her, and you should, too."

"You're all nuts," Drew sneers. "Why didn't you go to the police if Mom was doing such a thing?"

"I didn't have the proof they needed."

Drew smiles an *aha* smile. "See? Because there is none."

I rub the back of my neck, feeling a building pressure

there. One, I suspect, is coming from Drew's anger. "Dr. Hurley, it's time to take your son and leave."

Howard looks startled. "But I want to talk to Kit."

"Not with Drew present."

Drew points at me. "Shut up. This is none of your business."

Logan saunters in, Helen on his heels. "Drop that finger," he says in a calm, icy tone. "Or I'll break it. And then I'll escort you off this property with a swift kick to your backside."

Brax drapes an arm around me, gently steering me away from the angry man in front of me. "And once you're off this property," he says over the top of my head, "I'll do worse than that."

Drew is a big guy, but he can see the conviction in both of their faces. Logan takes my hand and pulls me to him, Brax following, the three of us forming a wall in front of Kit. Helen peers at the group, as if she believes we have truly lost our minds, but she's ready to put her foot down regardless. "Young man, your father has always spoken highly of you, and I respect him a great deal, but I can assure you it's in your best interest to leave, right now, or along with Logan and Brax following through on their threats, I'll be calling the police."

The final straw. Helen Cross is a petite thing but the metal in her voice makes everyone stand taller and keep quiet. No matter where she goes, or who her audience is, it's one of the things I always admire about her. She has a strength born of generations, and her bravado is backed by her power in this town.

"Come on, Dad." Drew gestures for his father to join him. "Let's get away from these small-town losers."

Howard stands his ground. "You go. I'm staying."

I flick my gaze to Kit and see that she's torn. She wants to talk to him, but she's leery of what Drew might do. I am as well.

"Why don't you and your son return to the hotel," I suggest. "You have things to discuss. When you're done, Howard, swing by The Wedding Chapel. I'm sure we'll be up. You and Kit can talk in private there."

He glances her way, as if seeking permission. "Go on," she tells him. "And if you can't come by later, call me. I'll be awake."

Drew starts to say something, but Howard grabs him by the arm and pushes him out. We wait for them to leave, not speaking until we hear their respective cars drive away.

Helen rounds on me. "Are you going to tell me what this is all about?"

As if it's my fault? The ghosts are still absent. Could I be lucky enough that they've moved on without my assistance?

Doubt hangs on me, but at least the pressure of Drew's anger is gone. I lean against Logan's shoulder and enjoy the feel of him rubbing my back in reassuring strokes. "I think it's time for us to leave," I tell her. "Tomorrow is a big day."

I expect her to argue, demanding to at least know what was going on between Howard and Kit, but Logan intercepts any argument she might make. "It was a wonderful night, Mother. Thank you for everything you did."

He kisses her cheek, holding my hand to lead me out. The others follow. "Yes," I say. "Thank you for everything. I know the reception is going to be perfect."

I can see by the look in her eyes she doesn't believe that.

Unfortunately, neither do I.

The morning of my wedding dawns cloudy, a fine mist falling as I sit on the back porch, enjoying my tea. I imagine the ever-negative Clarice is having a smug time of it.

Tabitha and Samuel wave at me from the farmhouse. Neither has spoken to me, seeming to be wrapped up in their own world. Maybe that's good.

The weather is supposed to clear by lunch, and I'm feeling optimistic about the day, regardless of the fact I can't see the sunrise.

Logan and I went to bed before midnight, but I woke sometime later, hearing Kit's soft chuckle. Howard dropped by around ten and the two snuck off for a walk. They returned and disappeared out here. I'm dying to know what happened, but my nosiness will have to wait.

I hear Logan making breakfast, Arthur and Lancelot keeping him company. Moxley, however, has joined me as per normal, and he stares down the hill toward the stream. He barks once, and I follow his line of sight, seeing Gilbert appear. Our eyes meet and he smiles before disappearing inside the farmhouse. I wonder how Samuel and Tabitha will take this new turn of events.

I'm sipping my tea when Persephone pops in, startling me. Warm liquid spills down the front of my nightgown, and I hurriedly brush at it with a napkin, setting the cup aside. "Good morning," she says. "Sherlock and I will see you at the church, but I wanted to stop by and wish you well."

I toss the napkin next to the mug. "I appreciate that. Thank you for your help yesterday when I was caught in the time fractal."

"Kit's the one who made the door for you. You should thank her."

"I'll do that. You and Sherlock getting along okay?"

She glances across the lawn, staring at the farmhouse. "Today may not go exactly how you wish, but it will all work out for the best."

"Sounds cryptic. Does this have something to do with Samuel?"

"He's in good hands," is all she says before she disappears again.

She claimed he'd received an extension. Had something changed overnight? I make a mental note to be sure I talk to him before everything gets too crazy. I told him I wouldn't force him to cross until after this event, but I may not be the only party who has a say in it.

I finish my drink and Logan calls me in. Kit joins us, looking happy for the first time in days.

"I take it your conversation with Howard went well?" I hand her the plate of toast.

She takes a slice to butter. "It was good to talk to him. There's a lot of emotional garbage between us that needs resolving, and I don't think Drew will ever accept me. We'll just have to see where it goes."

Logan cuts his egg. "I hate to bring this up, but the other day when I spoke to him, he warned me to stay away from you. That you were bad news. What happened between then and now?"

"When he said he was having a hard time wrapping his mind around all of this, it wasn't simply about the past. He got a call from Regina yesterday morning, and he went to her house. She claimed the bathtub drain pipe was plugged, and the contractor couldn't get there for days. Of course, he doesn't want anything to do with her, but she *is* the mother of his son. Sometimes, he gives in and does things for her to keep the peace." She tops the toast with a fried egg and adds cheese before smashing all of it under another slice. Her sandwich looks pretty good, and now I'm wondering why I didn't make one, too. "While he was there, she got a call and went outside to take it. He cleared out the clump of hair, realizing she wasn't lying about the drain pipe, but knowing how devious she is, he wondered if she hadn't created it herself. She has a new cat, and he heard the thing knock something over in the other room and screech bloody murder, so he went to investigate. He couldn't believe what he found hidden behind a secret door the feline had knocked open—all kinds of witchcraft items, including spells she had printed from the Internet. There was a vial of what looked like blood, and other things that sort of freaked him out. Feathers and bones, a voodoo doll, half-burnt candles. She had a clump of hair, cuttings from fingernails, all kinds of stuff."

I swallow my bite of egg. "She's a witch?"

"Or at least playing at it. I reached out psychically to see if I could pick up her energy, and mostly what I got was a lot of static interference. I sensed magic, but it was mixed up. Different kinds, different belief systems, I think she's just..."

"A New Age, wannabe," I supply for her. "Sage says there are a lot of those around."

"As he mentioned, he never found actual proof of the poisoning. Yesterday in that room? He found information about poisonous household products, and even worse, how to use them to kill someone over time and go undetected."

"Did he call the police?" Logan asks.

She takes a bite, chews, and swallows. "And say what? Again, it's proof to him, but not anybody else. There was nothing that pointed to her confessing that she had tried to off him, nor to say she was trying to do it now."

I sip coffee. "Does Drew live with her?"

She shakes her head. "But they're close. He spends a lot of time at her house."

My mind turns that over. "You don't think she would try to poison him, do you?"

A derisive laugh escapes her lips. "He's her whole world. She would never hurt him."

"Who else might be a target?"

A shrug. "No clue."

We finish eating. I take Kit's plate and set it in the sink. "You should share this with Sage, and see what she thinks."

"I'll do that now. Then I'll be back to help with whatever you need for today."

"Everything's under control, so far," Logan says.

"But the day is young," I add with a wink. "Plus, Persephone made some cryptic statements this morning that have me wondering about all kinds of things that could go wrong."

Logan rubs my arm after drying his hands. "Nothing can

come between us, so it doesn't matter. Whatever happens, happens. We'll deal with it."

Kit disappears and he kisses me, long and slow, bending me backward, his arms around me.

I'm out of breath when we pull apart. "You're absolutely right. First of all, we're already married. Secondly, a ring and a piece of paper do not determine our commitment to each other. All this fanciness, this show, isn't for us. This is for our family and friends. This should be our day, but it's theirs. I know you're mine, and I'm definitely yours."

Mama and Daddy arrive, and shortly after that, it's a parade of people coming and going, phones ringing, gifts being delivered from out-of-town guests. Jenn, her sister, Penn, and their husbands go to the estate. She video calls me, moving her cell around to prove how everything is in place to ease my mind. "We're a go," she tells me. "See you at the church."

She swings it again, and Penn waves at me. Their spouses give a halfhearted nod, and Jenn turns the camera back to her face. "This is going to be epic."

I sure hope so.

Rosie arrives after following up with the florist, photographer, Reverend Stout, and our ushers. Her cheeks are flushed and her eyes are bright. "This may be the biggest event we've ever done."

"Probably so," I agree. "Is Queenie set?"

She scans her list. "She's at the estate ordering everyone around in the kitchen. Even Helen skedaddled to get away from her."

Logan chuckles. "That's good for her."

Lia arrives, flashing a Cheshire cat's grin. For once her hands are free, and there's no backpack filled with ghost-hunting equipment on her shoulders. She's dressed in a pastel sheath, and she's tamed her wild curls with a matching bandanna. "I hope you like the gift I got you."

"I'm sure I will."

She doesn't give me any other hint, doesn't whip out a present from a hidden spot inside the house, so I pull Rosie aside after the girl heads to my office. "Do you know what she's talking about?"

Rosie makes a zipping motion over her lips. "I'll never tell."

Braxton and Rhys arrive, and I am hustled upstairs. An hour later, my hair and makeup are done and my nails are fabulous. When I walk back downstairs, everyone has left. Brax carries the garment bags with my dress and Logan's tux through the front door, telling us our outfits will be waiting when we arrive.

"Where did they all go?" I ask Logan.

He takes me in his arms. "I requested to have a few minutes alone with you before we head to the church."

"I can't think of a better wedding gift."

The clouds have cleared, and someone has left sandwiches for our lunch. The morning went by so quickly, I can't believe we're only a few hours away from the big event. I never had a chance to speak to Samuel, but he'll have to wait. I just hope nothing has changed about him hanging around a while longer.

"How's your mother?" I ask as we lounge in front of the fireplace with the food. While the embers are quiet, and the house is warm, I look forward to the next time we sit here, the ceremony done, and our future stretching in front of us.

Mox and the cats join us, sniffing the air because of the sandwiches. Logan extends his long legs, propping his feet on the coffee table. "I checked on her a while ago and she was complaining, but it was in that Helen Cross way. She loves every minute of this."

We share a knowing smile. "What about Winston? I don't want him messing things up, but I also can't confront him about Brianna and Kit yet."

"I have the feeling Mother is keeping him far too busy for him to cause trouble."

I hope so. "I'll do everything I can to keep any ghosts from interfering."

He draws me close. "I know this is tough for you to do, but don't stress about it. Like you said, today is for our friends and family. I want you to enjoy it, too. For a few hours, I want you to be free of the responsibilities on your shoulders. That includes the earthbound spirits. I've already spoken to Sherlock and your grandfather. I'm sure they were listening. I might not be able to kick ghosts out of our reception, but they can. Anybody harasses us, living or dead, and they'll find themselves in hot water."

A huge smile crosses my face. "I love you."

His watch alarm goes off and he glances at the time. "I love you, too. Let's get this show on the road."

I say goodbye to the cats, and he hooks Moxley to his leash. We've chosen to walk to the church, like we normally do, rather than take the car. The grass is still wet from the morning mist, but the road is clear and the sidewalks are dry. Moxley has to stop a few times to mark his territory and sniff, but we arrive right on time.

In the dressing room, Mama and Gloria are waiting for me. "Would you like help getting ready?" Mama asks.

There are tears in her eyes that she keeps trying to brush away. I didn't want anyone besides Gloria to see me in the gown until I walked down the aisle with Daddy, but now I remember the words that I said to Logan moments ago. "That would be wonderful." This has been a long time coming, and she's been very patient with me waiting for it. If she wants to be here to help me get ready, that's fine with me.

The two women chat nonstop as we get everything situated. The dress fits like a dream, and the three of us stare at my reflection. Once I'm zipped up, Mama's trembling hand goes to her lips. "Oh, Avalon. You've never been more beautiful."

The woman staring back at me in the mirror is somewhat of a stranger. Even when I'm in full business attire and wearing lipstick, I look nothing like this.

It's only my eyes that seem the same. Normal. They're Mama's. Aunt Willa's. "I bet you looked like this on your wedding day," I say to her.

She turns me so she can gently place her arms around me and give me a hug. "All I've ever wanted is for you to be happy."

"I am, and I want this day to be as special for you and Daddy as it is for me."

She steps back, hanging onto my shoulders as she looks me over. "I'm glad Logan makes you happy."

Gloria gives her my veil. "Would you like to do the honors?"

Carefully, she secures it on my head and drapes the front panel over my face to check that it's centered. I blink and my pulse jumps, the white, lacy fabric creating a similar sight to when I time-ride. Everything in me freezes for a moment, their voices fading out, and my world going monochrome.

But then she's lifting the fabric off my face and securing

it in place, and the world comes back into color, their voices normal once more.

Shaking slightly, I laugh and try to relax. I'm being paranoid. "I think I'll go without it," I say. "It will show off my hair better." I wink at Mama before she can question the decision. She shrugs and removes it as I ask, "Is it time?"

As if on cue, I hear the organ. Mrs. Stout is starting up the Vivaldi piece I've chosen to proceed the famed bridal march.

Gloria smiles and air kisses my cheeks. "Thank you for letting me sew your dress. I wish you a long, joyous life with your chosen."

She disappears out the door, leaving me and Mama. "Well, I guess I better get to my seat."

Samuel becomes visible at that moment. Although he's in spirit, he plans to join me and Daddy. I give him a quick smile, then ask her, "Would you walk with me?"

"Your father is doing that."

"You can take the other side." Samuel will have to bring up the rear. He nods his understanding.

Mama is a traditionalist, and I see the argument forming in her eyes, but then she presses her lips together. "I'd like that."

Samuel hovers at the door, his ghostly attire from the 1700s seeming perfectly normal to me. She links her arm with mine, handing me my bouquet. Down the hall and around the corner, we find Daddy. His face lights up when he sees us, and Mama hurriedly explains in a hushed voice that I've asked her to accompany me, too. He holds out his arm, and I put my free one through it. "That's a great idea," he says. "My two favorite ladies. I'm a lucky guy."

The three of us pause under the arch to the nave, and

Mrs. Stout signals the congregation with a long chord. They rise and turn en masse.

Logan and Chuck are at the end on one side, Moxley at Logan's feet. Brax and Rosie are on the other. Hundreds of faces stare at me, but I lock my gaze on my soulmate. The next few minutes go by quickly, and, although we've practiced our vows, I get all choked up, feeling the love from those gathered, a few of them in spirit.

Even Aunt Willa shows. When Logan and I are pronounced husband and wife, the smile she gives me is priceless.

So is the kiss Logan lays on me before we turn around and the crowd cheers.

Tabitha, in cat form, trots out from under the organ and slinks about my ankles, rubbing against my gown. We're about to make our way down the aisle once more, and I hiss at her, "Don't get hair on my dress!"

Samuel laughs. Several people frown and exclaim over the cat, but I ignore them and use my foot to gently push her aside. She looks up at me with a cheeky grin and begins cleaning one paw.

Outside, we go to our waiting limo. Birdseed is thrown, good wishes are called, and we hug and kiss our parents before we climb in.

I pick seeds from my strands, laughing as the driver peels away from the curb. "We did it."

Logan helps me. "The first hurdle complete, and may I say, that dress is stunning."

"By the way your mouth fell open when you saw me, I assumed you liked it."

He nuzzles my neck, sending shivers down my spine. "I don't just like it, I love it."

"You don't look bad in that tux either." I tug at his tie.

There's a teasing, sexy glint in his eyes. "You know, we could stop at home before we go to the estate."

I've seen that look before. He has something in mind that involves a lot fewer clothes. "Be late to our own reception?"

"Driver," he calls. "We need to make a pitstop."

I laugh as his lips find my neck again and we head for the house.

TWENTY-EIGHT

Even with our sideline activities, we're only half an hour late. No one seems to have noticed our absence. The DJ is playing, people are drinking, and the dance floor is full.

The photographer hustles us to the garden, and we begin a series of poses as instructed, some of the two of us, others involving our families and attendants. Tabby appears again and she and Moxley get in plenty of shots. Samuel, Persephone, and even Sherlock do as well, but I'll be the only one who sees them in the final prints.

When that's over, Logan goes to get me a drink, and Rosie leads me to the spot we picked for me to throw the bouquet. Jenn is busy gathering the single women, calling them to gather around us. By the time Logan returns with a cup of spiced cider, there's a considerable crowd. After I gulp half the beverage, he assists me onto the bench and I smile at them. "Who's ready?"

A cheer goes up, along with many hands. The photographer tells me to wait a moment while he gets into position, using a chair to elevate himself so he can obtain a shot with everyone's faces in it. He tells me to hold the arrangement above my head as if I'm about to throw it, then peers through his lens and calls orders to those in the group. None seem to mind adjusting their positions or shifting their heads, but their focus is on the bouquet.

Betty did a lovely job and it's so pretty, I hate to toss it away. As I usually suggest to brides, I had her make an identical one that I can keep. Many of the bachelors in the crowd have now congregated a ways back, watching the ladies and their excitement. Lia rushes forward, toting her camera. "Wait!"

I eye the camera. "What are you doing?"

She adjusts her glasses and looks all around before she meets my eyes. "I'm live streaming."

"You're *what*?"

"Lots of people who didn't get to come. You're like royalty around here, and I figured the folks who aren't here might want to see you take your vows and enjoy your reception."

I suddenly feel self-conscious. Kit appears, staying out of the scene and grinning. "I think it's a marvelous idea."

I narrow my eyes at her. "You should have talked to me about this."

Lia shakes her head. "That would've blown my surprise."

"Plus, you would've said no," Kit adds.

"*This* is your gift?"

Enthusiastic nodding ensues. "Pretty cool, huh?"

"Cool." *Kill me now.* "Right."

The photographer catches my eye. "I've got the perfect

shot, but your group is chomping at the bit. They're not gonna stand there forever."

I understand his impatience; the women are restless. I place my back to them once again, ignoring the idea that I'm on a live feed, and whisper a blessing on the flowers. Then I take a wild swing and toss the bouquet.

A cry goes up, then a collective gasp. I turn to find a stunned Kit standing there, staring dumbfounded at her hands.

"Did you see that?" Lia is beside herself. "It did a left turn right in midair. Gosh, I hope I got that."

She swings the camera around to Kit. Kit, still speechless, raises her gaze from the flowers to me. She shakes her head. "No. Here, toss it again." She strides over, holding it out. "I don't want it."

If we weren't live streaming, I might give her a hard time about it. "Why don't *you* toss it?"

"I'm not the bride."

I accept the bouquet, and she scurries away, heading for the barn and probably a stiff drink. Logan chuckles.

"Okay," I say. "One more time."

The photographer grumbles, reciting instructions to the clamoring women to return them to a decent position for his shot. I do the toss, and a young woman catches it this time. She's congratulated by a few friends, but most of the ladies trail away, disappointed. As the crowd disperses, Lia follows Logan and I. "Say something for the camera. For your fans."

He's used to a certain amount of fame in this town, and he smiles into the camera. "I married my best friend today." He faces me. "I look forward to everything the future brings our way."

Before I know it, he brings his lips to mine and gives me a

long kiss, bending me like he did earlier in the kitchen. If I didn't know better, I'd say he's been practicing this move.

Lia is ecstatic and runs off to film something else as he and I make our way to the barn. Rosie is waving at us. Night has fully fallen, and Queenie is directing servers there with large trays and covered containers. "It's time for dinner, you two."

"Yes, ma'am," Logan says.

He sits on my right, Brax on my left. I realize as we're served our meal that I haven't spotted a ghost yet. Honestly, I haven't been looking for any, but they usually show regardless.

As I dig into the delicious food, all the people I love surrounding me, I enjoy the feeling of peace. Maybe Persephone pulled some strings with The Big Guy, or Aunt Willa is making sure the spirits behave. Either way, I'm grateful.

We finish, and Daddy, Brax, and Chuck give speeches. Logan and I share the first dance, him dipping me at the end. "Did you secretly take ballroom dance lessons?" I whisper as I stare into his eyes.

"When I was thirteen. Mother made Chuck and I both take them."

I bet he hated it, but I'm pleased that he's such a smooth dancer.

We dance some more, everyone flooding the floor we have set up that blinks with lights. Noah, the DJ, plays several fast songs and then slows it down. Daddy cuts in and Logan hands me over to him for a father-daughter dance. As he moves me about, I notice Noah hitting on Raven. He leans a hand on the table she shares with Sage and Kit, and grins at her. She crosses her arms. He persists, crouching beside her, and motioning at the crowd. Is he asking her to dance?

Another couple cuts off my view of them, but when I can once again watch, I see her pull out her phone and show Noah something. He shakes his head and she sets it down, turning her face away.

Giving up, he walks, shoulders slumped, back to the raised platform and cues the next song. A few bars in, he stops it, and the crowd moans, glancing at him. "We have a request," he says, pointedly meeting Raven's gaze. "This one is for you."

The heavy beat of a Beyoncé song bounces through the speakers. A bunch of the younger gals hoot and race to the dance floor. Lia dives into the center of the group, laughing and streaming.

Sage pokes her sister and Raven stands, sending a cool gaze Noah's way. He grins. She lifts her chin and joins the others. When I glance at Noah again, he's doing a poor job of suppressing a smile.

After that, it's time to cut the cake, and I'm tickled to see Howard join Kit at the table. Surprisingly, I haven't seen Winston. I assume Helen is keeping him busy and he's in charge of the house staff.

Logan and I feed each other slices of delicious lemon cake with a raspberry layer and Queenie's famous silky frosting. It's so good, I close my eyes and moan. Logan has a smear in the corner of his mouth and I gently wipe it off, grinning. He catches my hand, kissing my palm. We entwine our arms to drink champagne and Logan places his flute to my lips.

The bubbles hit my nose, and just as I'm about to drink, Bobby V and Randall Grimes appear behind him.

Grimes is gripping the gun from Nettie's room.

TWENTY-NINE

I gasp and champagne goes everywhere but my mouth.

"Ava." Logan sets down the flute and reaches for napkins.

I look at the gangsters, legs weak. I think about how strong Nettie was, how she could move physical objects. "What do you want?" I ask Grimes.

The crowd is murmuring, and Logan brushes the napkin against my dress. "Ghosts?" he asks quietly.

I nod. Grimes sneers. "You took her away from me."

"Who?"

"That maid. She screwed up my life, and I want revenge. Now she's gone, and it's your fault."

That's why he was still here. Because of her. "You had your chance. The only way for you to get to her now is to cross to the afterlife."

The people closest to us are wide-eyed, but mostly silent, listening. Others point and ask each other, "What's going on?"

I ignore all of them. Grimes' weapon is trained on Logan.

"Persephone."My voice is an order. A command. "Now." To my husband, I say, "Please don't move."

Samuel and Sherlock appear. "We'll take care of them," Samuel says.

But can they do it before Grimes gets off a shot?

Bobby V scowls at me. "You took my Maria Grace, too. I didn't even get to say goodbye."

"Why didn't you find her after you sent her away? Did you know she had the baby?"

His mouth falls open. "Boy or girl?"

Grimes elbows him. "That's not important." He moves the gun closer to Logan's head. "An eye for an eye. You took what was mine, now I take what's yours."

Samuel lunges for him, Sherlock for Bobby. I tackle Logan, and in the same breath, the gun fires.

The bullet punches into my shoulder and I cry out as we hit the floor. Logan wraps his arms around me, rolling us so he's on top, his frantic gaze searching for the source of the gunshot. I feel like I'm suffocating, the world going surreal. *A ghost just shot me.*

The crowd erupts in chaos, people screaming, plates and glasses crashing to the floor. The next thing I know Winter is peering down at me. I blink, fearing I'm hallucinating and she and Logan pull me to my feet. My friend, who is supposed to be in Oregon, chants something under her breath. "They're never done with you, are they? Don't worry, I've made us invisible."

She has perfected those spells. How many times has she told me that ghosts are easy, people are hard? Maybe for her, that's true. "What are you doing here?"

Logan is checking my arm and dialing 911 at the same time. "You need an ambulance."

Winter keeps hold of my hand. She's wearing a deep sapphire blue dress, her wild curls spilling over matching combs. "Don't let go of me. The only way the spell works is if we stay in contact. I came to surprise you, and instead, you're surprising me."

My husband frowns, slapping a napkin against my torn, bloody arm. "What just happened here? Who shot you?"

I grimace as he applies pressure. "Bobby V and Grimes. They're here." I glance around but don't see them. Kit rushes to us. "They're upset because I crossed Nettie and Maria Grace. They were going to kill you in an act of revenge."

His horrified expression is the last thing I want to see on our wedding day. "So you stepped in front of the bullet? Ava, what were you thinking?"

"You would've done the same." There's so much blood. I feel sick to my stomach, lightheaded. "I think I need to sit." They guide me to a chair.

"Where did they go?" Logan asks.

"Samuel and Sherlock tackled Bobby and Grimes," I tell him. "Do you think...?"

Winter moves so she's shielding me along with Kit as Logan continues to hold my arm. "That they took care of them? I certainly hope so."

Howard calls Kit's name, frantically searching for her as people jet back and forth. She chews her bottom lip. "Poor guy. He was just starting to come around to the idea that this stuff is real. He'll never recover from this."

Winter brushes a strand of hair behind her ear. "You don't look good, Ava. We should get you to the house so you can lie down."

Mama and Daddy push through the exiting crowd, calling for me. They must've been down at the lake, walking around when they heard the gunshot. "Avalon?" Daddy yells. "Where are you?"

"I need to let them know I'm okay," I tell Winter.

"Where is that ambulance?" Logan growls.

Winter seems torn, but she releases her grip. All of us come into view, and my parents hustle toward us, demanding answers.

Howard shakes his head and walks backward toward the open door. Outside, it's total mayhem, guests yelling, vehicles peeling out of the lot, and Helen shouting orders.

"I'm okay," I tell my mother and father, stomach queasy. "I just need to..."

The world goes white and my body feels suspended in the air, falling, and yet not reaching the ground.

I hear a rough laugh and a full-sized woman with dark, leathery skin and long hair squints at me. Her hand is out, pale and gray, as if she is reaching into the in-between to grab me from some other time fractal. "There you are," she says, her voice like water over marbles. "Where is your friend?"

Hot bile rises in my throat. I know without a doubt who this is. "Brianna."

Another laugh that raises the hair on my arms. "Did you like my wedding gift?"

I shake my head confused. "What?"

Her gaze flicks to my injured shoulder. "Those men have been waiting decades, one for vengeance and the other to find his lost love. Their anger and desperation were a beacon for me. You enraged them, and it grew stronger. But it's not you that I want."

Kit. "Why?" I can barely get the word out, my throat closing. I'm scared to move, afraid I won't be able to get back to my rightful time and place if I do. Her hand is coming far too close for comfort, though. I have no idea what she'll do if she can grab me. "What do you want with her? Did someone hire you?"

"Hire me?" She scoffs. "Rage is a powerful emotion, wouldn't you agree? So powerful. A woman scorned is a natural portal for it."

Everything clicks. "Howard's wife? Is that who's behind this? What did she offer you?"

"What can a human possibly give me that would make me do their bidding?"

The way she says it, it gives me pause. "You're right. She couldn't buy, or manipulate you, could she? You've already crossed over." I think of the items Howard found at Regina's. "She's trapped you, hasn't she?"

She steps fully into the in-between. "This place... I don't like it here."

"Yeah, well, me neither, but here we are. I can help you. I can undo the binding, whatever she used. Kit can help, too. She and my other friends are very powerful, they can break whatever hold she has on you."

"She won't like that." Brianna smiles, showing rotten teeth. "And I did receive some benefit."

"How can it compare to peace in the afterlife?"

"You don't know what I've seen, what I've experienced."

I feel a tug on my hand and I glance down to see someone intertwining their fingers with mine. Kit appears on my right side.

"This isn't too creepy," she says with a shudder. "Let's get out of here."

Brianna smiles. "There you are. I've been searching for you."

The hand that had previously been reaching for my

chest now moves toward Kit. "No!" I scream, knocking it away.

The motion sends me to my knees. My heart leaps, even as Kit clasps me harder, refusing to let go. It's only then that I realize Winter is holding Kit's other hand. I hadn't seen her. She snaps her fingers and Brianna stumbles back.

I hit the ground, cold and hard. The night is dark around me, but the world is no longer washed out. Brianna is gone.

Insects sing, the hoot of an owl echoes nearby, and the sounds of people coming and going grow louder. Kit, Winter, and I are lying on the vineyard's front lawn, fall decorations in a tattered heap around us. It appears we've landed on them.

I suck in air, half laughing with relief and half crying because of my ruined reception, my burning shoulder. My bloody gown.

Logan yells my name, sprinting across the distance between us. Others follow, but my brain is overloaded. All I can think about is where Brianna went. Where Bobby V and Grimes are.

Persephone comes into view at my feet. She nods at Winter and Kit. "That worked. She's back where she belongs, and luckily, so are all of you."

"What did you do?" I ask.

Winter extends a hand but Logan reaches us, sweeping me up and setting me on my feet, looking me over. "Where did you go? I couldn't find you. You just disappeared."

"She's okay," Kit tells him, patting his arm. She touches her temple. "I've seen it."

He hugs me to him, and I feel my knees go weak. "Thank goodness."

Sirens split the night. "Brianna is taken care of, but what about the gangsters?" I ask. "Are we sure they're gone?"

Tabby strolls out from behind a pumpkin and meows. Samuel appears. "We handled them."

Sherlock pops in next to Persephone. "That's the most fun I've had in a long time."

"Did you get them to the afterlife?"

Sherlock gives a confident, proud nod. "Bobby and Maria Grace have been reunited. They said to tell you thanks. Raymond is getting his comeuppance, and I have to say Nettie is pretty happy about it."

Kit and Winter laugh. I sigh. The ambulance, along with a police car, turns into the long drive, blue lights winging over us. Mama and Daddy join us, as well as Helen and LC, come running. Everyone is shouting questions at me, and I cringe. I'm too dizzy and weak to figure out plausible explanations.

I look up into Logan's face, my vision beginning to tunnel to a small circle. "I think I need to lie down now, for real."

He scoops me up like the bride I am and carries me across the lawn.

THIRTY

I never imagined I'd spend part of my honeymoon in the hospital.

The ER is so busy when we arrive, I'm placed in a surgical room, even though I don't require any. The doctor on call inspects my wound, wraps my arm, and pumps me full of painkillers and antibiotics. "You're lucky the bullet missed the bone and brachial artery. It's more than a scratch, but it should heal fairly quickly."

Detective Jones tries to take my statement when he's finished with Logan's. I'm loopy from shock and the medications in my veins, and the doctor insists he leave me be until I'm more stable. I'm grateful for that. I honestly have no idea what to tell the detective.

My wedding dress is ruined.

Along with my parents, Gloria insists it can be repaired and the blood stains removed. I'm not sure there's a point. Every time I look at it, I'm going to see a gun pointed at the back of Logan's head.

Daddy is livid, as is Logan, but there's nothing they can do. There are no criminals to hunt down.

The rest of our family and closest friends drop in to check on me. Winter and Kit never leave my side, while Rosie, Jenn, and Lia attempt damage control for the business. At one point, I'm moved into a private room, thanks to the sway of Helen with the hospital staff. She has said little to me, her face grim and her movements sharp as she informed us that her time was better spent at the winery handling the cleanup.

I sleep for a while, in and out of a haze, grateful for the hospital gown, which is the farthest thing from my ruined dress. I wake at one point crying, nearly hysterical from the buildup of emotions over the past week. Logan, who's managed to replace his tux with clean clothes, holds me, reassuring and solid as always. He insists it's perfectly natural, even though I rage against the tears as much as I do the unfairness of what the ghosts have done.

Once my feelings run dry, I splash water on my face, ignore my red, puffy eyes and uncomfortable arm, and find enough anger and determination to ask Mama to bring me fresh clothes. Against the doctor's advice, I check myself out and demand to go home. Logan tells me to wait for him to bring the car around and to stay put in the room until he comes to retrieve me. I understand he's afraid to let me out of his sight, especially knowing how many earthbound spirits hang out here. It must be Persephone, Sherlock, and Samuel keeping them at bay—none have so much as peeked in at me.

Lia arrives, hugging me violently, while I try not to grimace, with tears in her eyes. "Good gravy, I was so scared for you."

An odd calm has come over me. I pat her on the back.

"I've had better days, but I'm all right. Do you understand now why I worry about you engaging with the spirit world?"

Her face is serious as she releases the bear hug and nods. "Yeah, I get it."

Detective Jones knocks on the open door frame. "I saw Logan. Before you go, I want you to know I will figure out who did this and put them behind bars."

He is as solemn as Helen and as steely as my father. "I appreciate the sentiment, but you won't find the culprit."

He lifts a dark brow and places his hands on his leather belt. He is in full uniform. "I am personally interviewing every guest that was inside that barn at the time of the incident. Somebody saw something, And I will have the shooter behind bars before sunrise tomorrow."

Lia keeps a hand on my arm. "You can't. It was a ghost."

I sag against the bed, feeling sick again, and rub a hand over my face. Jones and I have history when it comes to my mediumship and criminal activity. "He's no longer an issue, though."

His eyes are as hard and calculating as his face. "You're telling me that a ghost shot you?"

"He was aiming at Logan, but yes, it was a ghost."

From inside his jacket, he produces an evidence bag with the gun, and a second with the bullet that went right through my flesh. "This is a real weapon, and you're saying a phantom was able to pick it up, load it, and shoot you."

I shrug. "His name is Raymond Grimes, and he was a gangster during Prohibition and The Great Depression. As you know, some spirits are stronger than others. He's been hanging around here for a very long time, and he also had help from a very strong psychic witch."

Lia is nodding. "I got it all. I was live-streaming, and I watched it. You can see the gun materialize out of thin air."

"Live streaming?" He frowns down his nose at her. "You caught the culprit on video?"

"Well, sure. You can't see him, but you can see the gun."

He pockets the weapon and wiggles his fingers at her. "Give me the tape."

"It's digital, dude." She pulls out her cell and taps the screen. "I'll email the file. There. Done."

His phone buzzes. He reaches into his back pocket. "And how is it that you have my personal number?"

"You're in Ava's contacts."

I've always been impressed with the multitude of scowls in his repertoire. The current one goes Code Red, and he nearly growls when he speaks. "This is evidence in my investigation, so whatever social media you've uploaded it to, take it down. Now."

She sits next to me, lacing her fingers through mine, and squeezing my hand. "It was for our website, and I'm not stupid. I didn't upload it anywhere. I shut the live stream off as soon as everything went to the goats, and I was only going to use parts for reels and on our blog and YouTube channel."

Went to the goats? My head feels fuzzy and I rub my belly, trying to calm the flip-flopping it's doing. "YouTube? I thought you were doing a podcast."

"I am." She brightens. "While I was filming the reception, I thought about how much I love doing this stuff. I've got all the equipment, why not start a YouTube channel? I can do lives when we're ghost hunting!"

I'm too blown out to argue, so I don't. To Jones, I say, "I'll write up whatever official statement you need, but it was a ghost. There's no getting around that. In fact, if you do a search on Bobby V, the gangster, you'll find a local historian who has a website with photos of him with Raymond Grimes and his mobsters. I'm pretty sure I saw that gun in at least one of the pictures."

Jones shakes his head in total disbelief, yet total understanding as well. "I still have to go by the book and investigate every option."

He leaves us sitting there, and Lia gently touches my thick bandage. "I saved you some cake. When I'm sick or hurt, sugar always makes me feel better."

I put my good arm around her, and we tip our heads together. "Then the day isn't a total loss. Thank you."

AT HOME, we find everyone gathered in the dark backyard, including Tabitha, Sage, and Raven. Even Paris is there, and I see Samuel, Persephone, and Sherlock.

"Oh, cool," Lia says, ditching her shoes and running around barefoot. "Are we catching fireflies? I'm really good at it."

There aren't many of those left this time of year, but the magic that exists here helps everything live a little longer. The gazebo lights are on, casting the group in a filtered glow, shadows dancing around the edges of the circle. "Catching a ghost is more like it," I say.

Winter steps forward, still in her beautiful blue dress. "We've got this. Why don't you go lie down?"

I see distress in Kit's face, and can only assume Brianna is the reason. "You didn't get rid of her for good, did you?"

Winter offers a patient smile. "I'm a strong witch, but this is dark magic."

"Blood magic," Sage adds.

Winter continues. "Regina can call her back whenever she wants because she has a container for her. It's similar to possession. Brianna can't stay in it for long periods, but Regina doesn't need her to. What we have to figure out is a way to trap Brianna and break the binding between them, or Regina will use her to come after Kit again."

My legs are shaking, and I slump down on the gazebo steps. Logan gives a sigh of resignation, knowing he's not going to get me upstairs when all of my friends are here, making plans. "Drew is the container," I say, "isn't he?"

Kit nods. "His anger makes it easy for her to slip inside."

"There's also her ghost familiar," Raven adds.

A formidable threesome. But we have an equally formidable trio here. "Is there a way we can use one of them to draw Brianna into a sacred circle and break the tie between her and Regina?"

My grandmother sits beside me. "It's not a simple matter to break a blood binding. Brianna has already crossed to the other side and been brought back. That's one of the reasons she's so strong. Even if we destroy her favorite container, Regina can find another."

Destroy? I shiver.

Logan stiffens, understanding the meaning as well. "You mean as in kill him? That's definitely out of the question."

Tabitha fingers a piece of my hair, the wave completely gone now. There was blood on it until I rinsed it out, but I swear she can sense the residual of it. "We don't harm innocents. 'Tis his anger that makes him vulnerable and easy to control. If he'd give that up, that might do the trick."

"Fat chance, that," Kit snorts. "If Regina is willing to torture and use her son as her receptacle, who knows who else she might try?"

My brain longs for a break. My body aches for the comfort of my bed. "Howard told you about Regina having a vial of blood in her secret room. That belongs to Drew, right? Can we use that to break the binding?"

Sage sits in the grass, crossing her legs. Lia plops next to her. "Since she used that to create it in the first place, his blood would only strengthen it."

"What we need is Brianna's," Winter states.

Paris nods vigorously. "You could certainly use it to call her to you, and reverse-engineer the spell."

"She's a ghost," Logan says, as if we've all forgotten.

Magical logic. I can't quite wrap my mind around it. "If you reverse the spell, won't that make Brianna the master of Regina?"

Raven paces, fingering her necklace. I'm learning that she does this when thinking. "Not if we do it right. We use Brianna's DNA to override Regina's spell, granting Brianna freedom. She was dragged here unwillingly, even if she does like it."

Persephone snaps a finger. "She'll have to return to the afterlife. She isn't allowed to stay here unless granted special privileges, and she certainly hasn't earned those."

"There's one problem." I prop my elbows on my knees. "As Logan pointed out, Brianna's dead. We can't get her blood."

"And we don't know where she's buried." Paris rubs the back of her neck. "There is no digging up her bones, I'm afraid, to grab her DNA."

Logan brightens. "But we know someone who's related to her. If we get blood from him, would that work?"

Winter, Sage, and Tabitha exchange a look. "Between that and the spirit familiar, it might," Winter says. "We'll have to get her out of her favorite container before we do it."

Logan pinches the bridge of his nose. "Why do I have the feeling I'm going to be asking Winston for his blood?"

"I'll do it," Kit says.

"Are you sure?" I ask. "I doubt he's going to be cooperative. You better take Logan with you."

"I can handle him." She turns to the witches. "How do we trap the familiar?"

Tabitha grins. "Leave that to me, will ye? I'll handle the little ghost cat."

"That just leaves Drew." I glance at Logan. "Do you think you can lure him here?"

Before he answers, Winter says, "It would be better if we do it at Kit's. Transporting a ghost cat is difficult."

Logan rocks back on his heels, nodding. "When do you want him there?"

Sage checks her watch. "An hour?"

Kit rubs her palms on her thighs. "I'll hunt down Winston."

"What about us?" Sherlock inquires, pointing to himself and Samuel.

Gilbert becomes visible, making us jump. "Me, too."

Samuel whirls on him. "What are you doing here?"

I use the railing to help me stand. Tabitha takes my good arm to steady me. "You better get used to him hanging around, Grandpa."

"We haven't formally been introduced." Gilbert offers a hand to him. "I'm your new guardian angel."

My many-times great-grandfather sputters, then regards me, Persephone, and finally Tabitha with wide eyes. "I fear I do not understand."

Join the crowd. "The spirit world works in mysterious ways," I say. "Sometimes, as we say these days, you just have to go with it."

I head for the porch, and Lia rushes up to me. She and Logan stick close, as the others follow. I hear my cell ringing inside, and discover Mama calling. "We came back to the hospital and they said you went home."

"I'm okay," I assure her for the hundredth time. She and Daddy had gone to the vineyard to help with cleanup. "I'm going to bed shortly and will handle the fallout tomorrow."

I hate misleading her, but it seems to relieve her mind, and she sighs audibly. "We're here if you need anything."

"I know. Good night, Mama. I love you."

Daddy hollers, "We love you, too!"

There's a knock at the front door. The others are gathered around me and we exchange a look. It's after midnight. Who could it be? Not my parents, and I sure hope it's not Jones wanting another interview.

"I'll get it," Logan says.

At the sound of the man's voice on the other side when he answers, everything in me goes on high alert.

"Now's not a good time," Logan growls.

"I'm sorry to bother you, especially after what happened. How's Ava?"

On trembling legs, I walk to the foyer. Of all the people I thought might be standing on my doorstep, Drew Hurley is not one of them. "This isn't a casual visit to check up on me. What do you want?"

"Kit," he says with determination. "I have to talk to Kit."

THIRTY-ONE

She's next to me in a heartbeat. "Is your dad okay?"

"He's fine." He lifts a bag that seems weighted, holding it out to her. "I need..." He seems unable to find the words. "He told me about what Mom did—has done. Is doing. I didn't believe him, and I went to her house to prove he was lying. But I found the room. Found..." He swallows hard. "I think it's my blood, my nail clippings, my hair." His face is horrified and filled with hurt. "I don't understand any of this."

Kit reaches for the bag, but Tabitha is there, grabbing it instead. "Careful," she murmurs to my friend. Then to him, "Looks like ye have brought us a present. What's inside?"

Persephone has kept herself, Samuel, Sherlock, and even Gilbert, visible. They, along with my witchy friends, gather around, pressing in to look over our shoulders. Drew barely glances at any of them, swallowing hard and pointing at the bag. "I brought it, all of it. The spells, the vial, the other stuff that was on the table. I don't know what she was using it for, but I thought maybe you could tell me. You could explain this to me." His voice wavers on the last few words.

His aura is a muddy yellow and I feel sorry for him.

Kit places a comforting hand on his arm, understanding his distress and sympathizing with his desperation to make sense of all this. "Why don't you come in?"

Logan directs him to the sofa, the rest of us taking up spots in the room. Lia and the ghosts hang back, as does Persephone. Tabitha removes each of the items and lines them up on the coffee table.

My grandmother draws her finger in a circle over them, and I see her sparkling magic creating a bell jar over all of it. Smart, in case Regina has booby-trapped or placed a hex on them individually. One thing I've learned in this work is to never underestimate the enemy—even those with little experience and no inborn abilities sometimes get lucky.

For the next few minutes, Kit explains things to Drew, the others chiming in when he asks questions. He has a lot of those. "I just can't believe it," he says, disbelief evident in his stiff body posture, shaking head, and devastated but suspicious eyes. "She's my *mother*."

"I have no doubt she loves you," Kit says, her hand on his arm again. "Sometimes people get off on the wrong track, especially when they've been hurt. She's going down a dark path, and she's playing with things she doesn't have true comprehension of. With your help, we can break the bind she's created with the dead witch and perhaps turn things around."

She tried to poison his dad. I don't think there's any coming back from that, but I keep my mouth shut. Kit is offering Drew a lifeline when he desperately needs it.

He sits forward and scrubs his face. After a long moment, he appears to rally. "What do you need me to do? I don't want to lose her."

"The first thing," I say, too far gone to be polite, "is to lose the attitude toward Kit, and the anger you've been directing at her. I realize this is a lot for you and you're going to need time to work through it, but Kit is a kind, decent person, and she deserves respect. Your parents' marriage was already on the rocks when she met your father. That's when Regina started down this path and Kit tried to keep him safe. You should be thanking my friend, rather than taking out your disappointment over what happened between them on her."

He rears back as if I've slapped him. I'm not sorry for it. "I get that. It's just—"

"She's your mother," I supply. "I know. You found the evidence of what she's been doing, and you understand that your father would not make this up, right?"

He bobs his head, disgruntled but coming around to the facts that can't be denied. He flicks his gaze to Kit. "I'm sorry. If I hadn't been so tangled up in my hatred for you, which was not about you at all, none of this would've happened. This was about me. About my disappointment with both my parents."

She gives him a sad smile. "Your mother couldn't stand losing your dad, regardless of the reason, and her need to control him and their marriage led to this."

"And in the end, she still lost him."

Kit's cell dings and she reads the message. "Winston will meet us at my place in ten minutes. We better get going." She drags Drew to his feet. "You, too."

The big guy looks confused. "Me? Why?"

"You said you wanted to help."

"How?"

Logan slaps him on the shoulder, propelling him to the door. "I'll explain on the way."

THIRTY-TWO

We drop Lia at home at my insistence, and for once, she doesn't argue. She only asks that someone let her know how it goes. A few minutes later, we're ready for Winston when he arrives.

Kit ushers him in. "I'm glad you could get here so quickly."

"I was on my way home from the vineyard." He's surprised to see us. "Miss Ava. I heard you were okay, but it's good to see with my own eyes."

"Hard to keep a Fantome down."

He looks at Logan. "Your mother is quite a trooper. We got as much cleaned up as we could, and she sent me off. We'll work on it more tomorrow after church. Some of it we can't touch until the police release the scene. Do you know if they have any leads? It all happened so fast, it doesn't seem as though anyone knows exactly who had the gun."

"No leads yet," Logan says, "but the important thing is that everyone is fine."

He offers to get Winston a drink, but the butler shakes

his head. "I'm good." He turns to Kit. "You said there was something I could assist you with?"

She insisted that she wanted to take the direct route first. If he won't give us his blood willingly, then we have a backup plan. As she explains what has been going on, his eyes grow wider and wider, and he's speechless when she finishes.

Tabitha is in cat form, prowling the rooms, and I have yet to see the shadow familiar. I can feel it, though. It's so faint I wonder if Brianna's power is fading after what happened. Perhaps she was drawing energy from all of them—Grimes, Bobby, Nettie, and Maria Grace.

"I, uh, I don't know what to say." Winston sits back, sinking deeper into the couch. "I thought I was only related to Nettie."

Across from him in a rocking chair, I sit up straighter. "The maid? You didn't tell us that when you shared the story about her."

He looks chagrined, whether about not confessing that, or about being her kin, I'm not sure. "There are things in my family history I don't like to discuss, and truth be told, I'm not a hundred percent certain of it."

"Why not?" Kit asks.

"Long story." He picks at invisible lint on his pants. "A painful one."

"But if it's so, that means you're related to Maria Grace and her child," I say.

He hesitates, then lets go of a puff of air. "It's possible that she's my grandmother."

Stunned silence snakes through the room. "Bobby V is your grandfather?" I can't wrap my mind around it.

He shrugs, appearing embarrassed, as if sharing this secret is shameful. "No one ever figured out what happened to Maria Grace and her baby, but there was speculation. Some thought the two of them died, others said she ran away and had the baby in Arkansas. From the research I did years ago, it looked as if she might have had the child, but didn't survive the birth. There was a record found after the local doctor passed away that suggested she may have been one of his patients." Hope sparks in his face. "He delivered a child whose mother died, and he turned the baby over to the orphanage. The same orphanage Bobby V grew up in."

"The one he was famous for giving money to." I turn that over, but something Bobby said tells me the gangster never realized his child was there. Was it for the best? "He didn't know," I say. "He was totally surprised when I told him that Maria Grace had given birth."

"There's more." Winston pauses. "If it's true that I'm related to Brianna, she's not my cousin. She's my mother."

It's like water in our faces. Paris shakes her head. "That can't be. Our books are never wrong. If Brianna had a child, it would be listed."

"I can sympathize with having a wacko mother," Drew tells him. He's been so quiet, I've forgotten he was even here.

"Let me get this straight," I say. "Brianna is Maria Grace and Bobby V's daughter, and you're her son."

He worries his hands. "I had no idea any of this was going on." He peeks at Kit. "You said you were having trouble with your psychic abilities, but you didn't tell me Brianna was the cause. I mean, she didn't raise me. I barely remember her. She sent me to live with a couple who were childless. I grew up in a normal household—no magic, or psychic mojo."

A tangled web to be sure, but as I follow the threads, I see how they lead back to a single person—me. "The doctor who delivered Brianna is one of my ancestors." I eye Gilbert, who hasn't said a word.

Reluctantly, he steps forward. "Due to the times and the danger the doctor and the child might have been in, he buried Maria Grace on his property."

"Which now has the B&B on it," I supply.

The front door is thrown open, banging against the wall. We all jump. A woman I've never seen strides in and points a finger at Kit. "You," she sneers.

Drew leaps to his feet. "Mom?"

In her sharp gaze, I see a familiar ghost. "That's not your mom," I tell him.

The woman's red lips curl. Brianna's voice comes out of her mouth. "Hello, cursebreaker."

"Cursebreaker?" Persephone scoffs. "That's a new one, but I guess it's accurate."

From the corner of my eye, I notice Winter becoming invisible, even as Sage steps forward with her sister, the two of them gesturing in the air. A clear, but visible wall pops up between Regina and the rest of us.

Brianna, using her, chuckles softly. "They talk about you, you know, on the other side." She pays no attention to the wall, or the others, her focus solely on me. "The one who broke her family's curse, and the one on him." Her chin lifts toward Logan.

He steps in front of me as I stand. "You don't belong here, and whatever you think you're going to do to my wife, you've got another thing coming."

"Gilbert buried my mother like she was a piece of trash," she states. Her voice is low, calculating. She doesn't seem concerned about the wall, keeping Regina's body incredibly still—a cat about to pounce. That's when I notice her familiar slinking through the nearly invisible barrier, and positioning itself next to her. "It wasn't until I died that I realized what had happened to her, how she was stuck in the in-between because of him." Her finger points at Gilbert. "How my grandmother wouldn't cross either, because of what the good doctor did."

Drew is whipping his gaze back and forth between his mother's body and Gilbert. "Mom? What is happening?"

Over the top of Logan's shoulder, I hold her wrath-filled gaze. "But they're both on the other side now. Everything is resolved. Go back to the afterlife and leave us be. Gilbert did the best he could for her at that time. An unwed pregnant mother was not allowed to be buried in the Christian cemetery, and he was afraid for you. Afraid of handing you over to the gangsters. He did you a favor."

Her hands curl into claws. The cat hisses. Tabitha, while human, hisses back. Everyone's aura flares bright, an ocean of different colors—anger, fear, revenge, and protection. The pressure in the back of my neck builds and Kit grabs her head, letting go of a painful cry.

Brianna doesn't need Regina's form to get through the barrier. She can use her immense psychic abilities to do plenty of damage.

We need a magic circle to trap her, but there's no time. To Logan, I whisper, "I need my cross." To Brianna, I say, "You were the one pulling me into the in-between. It's not a new ability I have, you were dragging me there, weren't you?" Distraction is all I have, as Logan slides his foot to my bag lying near the chair. "You were causing me to see that horde of ghosts surrounding the property. An illusion."

"Maria Grace died without even seeing my face. Without seeing her mother again, or the man she loved. And then Gilbert tossed her in the ground without so much as a simple prayer. She couldn't cross, but neither could she see or hear in this world. All that time, wanting to find us, and not even knowing that she was dead. It drove her mad."

"No, it didn't." While she had been eager to find Bobby and go home to her mother, she'd been more sane than the spirit I currently faced. "But it did you. Maria Grace was stuck in a point in time, yes, but she had no concept of what had happened or the years that have passed since she died in childbirth. That's why she still believed she was pregnant and that Bobby was coming for her. She had hope, and she knew she was loved, just like she loved you. Now she's reunited with Bobby and Nettie, and at peace. All of them are, except you."

"I don't want to be reunited. I want revenge."

"My ancestor has been her guardian angel, watching over her while she was stuck. He may not have done things the way you believe he should have when he was alive, but he never left her. He didn't abandon her, as you claim he did."

She growls and the cat arches its back. Kit falls to the floor, curling in on herself and squeezing her head. The pressure in my neck ramps up, piercing into my skull. Logan shifts the purse close enough that I can reach it, shoving my hand inside and grabbing the iron cross.

Winston and Drew scramble away as Brianna, using Regina's body, rakes her nails through the barrier, shredding it.

I'm not afraid, only determined to stop her. With the wall disintegrating, I grit my teeth against the pain and blink back the lightheadedness tunneling my vision down until all I see are specks of her glittering aura. Stepping out from behind Logan, I throw the cross with every ounce of strength I have.

Time slows. The shadow cat leaps. Tabitha does as well, shifting with a pop in mid-air. They collide, a tangled ball of claws and fur. Winter becomes visible behind Regina, and as Brianna tries to recoil out of the path of the iron, Winter clamps an arm around Regina's waist and keeps both her and Brianna planted.

My aim is accurate, the cross frisbee-ing through the air and smacking Regina in the forehead. Her eyes roll skyward and she slumps in Winter's arms.

Brianna, knocked from her host, screams as the iron bites into her spirit body. Winter releases Regina and grabs the iron before it hits the carpet. She waves her other hand and a new barrier springs up around Brianna. A container of magic.

"My blood!" Winston shouts. He sticks out a hand. "Take it."

Logan draws his pocket knife. A quick slice of Winston's finger and the red life force flows.

Raven and Sage speak in unison, calling on angels and other spirits to assist them. Paris chimes in. Winter grabs Winston's finger and swipes it on the cross. Persephone directs and orders Sherlock and Samuel to join the circle outside the container holding Brianna. I stagger, and Logan catches me, easing me into the chair before he also joins them.

Drew drags Regina's body out of the way, kneeling next to her and patting her cheeks. I try to force myself to stand, to get to the circle, but like Kit and Regina, I am helpless.

Until Tabby and the ghost cat, fighting their way across the floor, bump into my legs.

Kit is still writhing on the ground. My head feels like it's about to explode, but I reach down, realizing the ghost cat is more corporeal than before. I'm dizzy, and when I grab for my bag, digging into it to find what I need, the room tilts. My stomach heaves.

Cool metal brushes my fingertips and I pull out the necklace. Cursebreaker. That's me.

As the two cats tussle, I hold onto the chair with one hand and wait for my opening. When it comes, I drop the necklace over the ghost familiar's head. "You are free now. Go to the light."

The pendant on the chain once held the spirit of a witch who had hexed it and would use it to harm Logan in retribution for what his mother's ancestor had done to her. I have kept it, not knowing why, only that it holds power. My power.

The ghost cat seizes, bellowing, and then a bright white light appears near the bookshelf. Brianna screams, "No!"

Too late. The cat floats toward the heavenly door, its body relaxing. It doesn't even glance her way, but it does look at me. Relief shines in its eyes, and then it's gone.

Winter holds up the bloody cross and lowers the barrier at the same time. "By all that's holy and right, I command you to return to the light." Her voice booms in the room. "Return to where you're supposed to be. Together, we set your spirit free."

Brianna fights, clawing at the air, screaming, but the pressure in the back of my head releases. I hit the floor on my hands and knees and crawl to Kit. As Brianna is forced into the light, Kit stops crying and grasps my arm when I reach her.

At the threshold, Brianna bellows at me. I owe her nothing, but I look up when she says, "Watch out, Cursebreaker. You haven't seen the last of—"

Winter holds up her open palm. "Yeah, yeah. We know. You're a powerful witch and you're going to come back and haunt us. Blah, blah, blah." She does a little wave and then closes her fist with a snap.

Brianna jets through the portal and it closes with a *thunk*. Winter lowers the cross and her hand, winking at me. "Spirits. Always trying to have the last word."

Raven chuckles. Sage's shoulders slump. My equilibrium returns, no more pressure or pain. My friend wraps her arms around my neck and cries into my shoulder with relief. A few tears slip from my own eyes, grateful that she is okay.

Regina revives and her son guides her to the couch. Her eyes are unfocused and she wobbles, gripping onto him for stability. "What happened? Where am I?" She glances at each of us. "Who are you people?"

Kit releases me, dashing away the tears and giving the woman an odd look. "You don't remember me?"

"Um, sort of? I can't place your name, though. Are you a professor at the college?" Her face is sickly, her lipstick smeared. She shakes her head as if clearing it from a bad dream. "I'm sorry. What am I doing here?"

"It's a long story."I take the hand Logan extends to me and allow him to help me stand. Together we get Kit on her feet.

"How long have you been dabbling in witchcraft?" Winter asks.

Regina blanches. "How do you know about that?"

I have the feeling Brianna isn't the first spirit to use her as a means to revenge. I lean on Logan. "I'm guessing it started when you and Howard began having marital problems. Am I right?"

She sucks in a sharp breath. "I may have tried a love spell or two." Holding up her palms in submission, she meets Drew's eyes. "I just wanted him to love me again."

"You tried to poison him," Kit says, defensive.

"Don't be ridiculous. I would never hurt him."

"She doesn't remember it," I say. "She was possessed."

"Brianna?" Winston asks.

"Not her, but someone else powerful."

"She may not be responsible for the bad things that she has done then," Tabitha says, once again in human form and naked as a jaybird.

I grab a throw blanket from the back of the sofa and wrap it around her.

Sage *tsks*. "That's why non-magical folks shouldn't mess with this stuff. You get yourselves in all kinds of trouble."

Regina frowns. "Non-magical?"

Raven points at herself, her sister, and Winter. "We're witches. Natural born, with plenty of abilities. Some of the others here are psychics."

"And even we don't mess with things that are out of our league," Sage adds. "No more downloading spells from the Internet, okay?"

"How do you know about *that*?" Her gaze bounces around. "And what do you mean by things that are out of my league?"

Drew pats her arm. He's obviously relieved that his mother is not a homicidal maniac. "Come on, Mom. We have a lot to talk about."

He leads her to the still-open door and turns once there. "Thank you for this. For giving me my mom back. And Kit?"

She leans heavily against me, worn out. "Yes?"

"I truly am sorry about everything. If you and Dad decide to try again, that's okay with me."

Her eyes flick to Winston, back to Drew. "Your father is a wonderful, kind man, but he and I have moved on. We're still friends, and that's a good thing. Tell him I wish him and your mom the best of luck."

Once the door closes, I hug her. "You think they'll reconcile?"

She taps the side of her head. "I know they will. That family is a hot mess, and they have a ton of healing to do, but they should do it far, far away from me."

Tired laughter echoes in the room. Each and every one of us is rung out, and we say our goodbyes, ready to leave this day behind. As Logan and I exit, I hear Winston say to Kit, "About that reading you were going to do for me…"

She chuckles under her breath. "You just want to know if I'm going to say yes."

A surprised pause. "I haven't even asked you yet."

"Sure you have. About a dozen times mentally. You've been practicing."

It's his turn to laugh. "And?"

"I think dinner and a movie would be great. How about Wednesday?"

We're in the car when I see Winston exiting, a crooked smile on his face. There's a matching one on Kit's as she leans against the frame, watching him.

THIRTY-THREE

Logan and I spend Sunday at home, never straying far from the bedroom. Food and drinks seem to materialize on their own outside the door and we don't question them. Between Persephone and Winter, as well as Tabitha and Samuel, I suspect we have more than one guardian angel watching over us.

When we finally emerge rested and ready to engage with people again, we find the house and yard empty. A small, wrapped box is on the kitchen table. Opening it, I discover a USB and a note from Lia. *Congratulations. Made this for you.*

Together, Logan and I help ourselves to glasses of wine in front of the fireplace, enjoying the flickering flames. I prop my injured arm on a pillow while he plugs the drive into his laptop and clicks on the single file it contains. We watch as our wedding day unfolds, starting here, then moving to the church, and the beginnings of the reception, up to—but not including— the cutting of the cake. At that point, it switches to interviews with friends and family. Short snippets about why they love us, their wishes for our future, and even a few random predictions about what that might hold.

It's easy to see which were filmed then, and those that have been filmed afterward, including one with Kit and Winston together. "Time is flexible," Kit says, "depending on our choices, and the ways we create karma for ourselves. Each of us has many potential paths we can choose to walk, and none of them are set in stone. I see a very bright future for the two of you." Her voice softens and she smiles. "I'm not going to tell you the juicy details, because I don't want to influence your choices, but as long as you're together, and you're true to yourselves as well as each other, I guarantee a happily ever after."

Helen is next, not nearly as cheery. "I should've known." She seems resigned, but not overly upset. This is good. "At least we got through the pictures. They turned out fabulous, by the way. I expect the two of you for dinner this week, so we can review them and choose the one for the announcement in the paper. You've provided the whole town with plenty of gossip." A big sigh. "While you've been holed up in your house, mine has become a ridiculous tourist attraction for true crime fanatics. Someone leaked a story about gangsters and revenge, and I'm fielding calls from a historian who's obsessed with Bobby Ventura. At least these freaks like to drink. The winery is doing a swift business. In fact, there's a line out the door, right now." Her attention snags off camera, then returns. "If this keeps up, I might break even on the expense of the reception. There's still plenty of leftover food if you want Winston to bring you some, and I went ahead and selected one of the wedding photos to sell, since you seem to have quite the fan base now. I know you won't mind, Ava." Such a simple statement that suggests I owe her, and this is how she is calling in her chip. I'm sure this won't be the only time. "Anyway, thank you for saving my son once again. Welcome to the family."

Logan and I are smiling and shaking our heads as the video continues and Jones appears, contrite and scowling. Big surprise. "Another unsolved case in my books," he grumbles, "but the important thing is, you're both alive. Do me a favor, and stay that way. I don't need any more paperwork."

Finally, Lia's sweet face closes out the recording. "You two are...some of the wildest but most legit adults I've ever met. Ava, I know you don't want to hear this, but it's true." She pauses, dragging in a deep breath. "I want to be like you when I grow up. Not the ghost-whispering stuff, although that's way cool. What I mean is, I want to help people. Have friends such as yours. The kind who know the real me and care about me anyway." I wasn't sure that was a compliment. "I want to be part of something bigger than just going to work every day and worrying about bills. I want to do something special with my life. That's why I keep trying all these different things. They're fun, and being your sidekick makes me feel important."

Logan glances at me. "Sidekick?"

"This is Lia," I say, which seems to explain everything.

On screen, she continues. "Anyway, I'm doing what you said and I'm going to work with Sage and Raven. Train. And study with Paris. She said I can visit her library anytime. I'm going to read all the magical books and see the kittens." A huge grin lights up her face. "I want to be involved in all of it —the magic, the ghosts, the event planning. But mostly, I just want to be your friend." She makes peace fingers at the camera, then uses the tips to pull her mouth down into a frown and back up in a smile. "Peace out, amigos."

The screen goes blank and Logan laughs. He sets the laptop aside and puts an arm around my shoulders. We settle deeper into the couch, the crackling blaze in front of us, soothing and, dare I say it, *normal.*

Moxley stands on his bed, turns twice, and resettles himself. Arthur and Lancelot drape their supple bodies over a chair, one on the arm, the other on the back. There are no ghosts, no guardian angels, and no other disturbances.

Peace.

I sigh and cross my ankles on top of the coffee table, snuggling against Logan's chest. "I could get used to this."

His thumb rubs tiny circles on the inside of my wrist. "Me, too."

We get a whole five minutes of this incredible normalness before Persephone interrupts it. "Ready?"

I close my eyes, trying to ignore her. "Go away."

Logan stiffens. "Who is it?"

"My annoying guardian angel," I grumble.

He downs the last of his wine as if girding himself. "What do you want, Persephone?"

She allows herself to be seen by him, sinking into the opposite chair from the cats and crossing her legs. She's wearing bell bottoms and a sweater with pumpkins on it. "I left you alone for twenty-four hours. You can't have all eternity."

I open my eyes and grin at Logan. "You're wrong. I've seen the future. I'm spending eternity with this guy."

I sense, more than see, her eye roll. "You have work to do."

I motion at Logan to pour us more wine while I bare my teeth at her. "Leave me alone. I'm on my honeymoon. Get back to me next week."

She grins. "I'm teasing. I just wanted to see that look on your face."

Her gloating form disappears, and we are once more alone. Glasses refilled, Logan raises his. "To us. The most legit adults around."

I know how lucky I am to have him. To have this life, even with the ghosts. I smile and clink mine against his. "And to our very bright and wild future together."

AVA AND LOGAN *will return in 2024 in Phantoms Are Forever. Be sure to sign up for my newsletter for the release date!*

And don't miss the new Candy Shop Witch series coming in 2024!

VISIT MY STORE

Did you know you can buy directly from me? When you do, the retailer doesn't take a cut and I can pass on the savings to YOU!

https://www.nyxhalliwell.com/books

Benefits:

You can find ALL my books in one place

SAVE money

EARLY access to new releases

Special Collections, Boxed Sets, and Limited Editions

Support a small business (and support a dream!)

Why Buy Direct?

When you purchase a book by your favorite author, electronic or print, on retailer platforms, the company keeps 30-70% of the sale, leaving the author with little to no profit (after the company deducts delivery fees, taxes, and other fees).

Buying directly from the author means that more goes to them so they can keep turning out stories for you. Every published story, every book, requires cover art, editing, and hours and hours of the author's time simply to create it. Not to mention overhead costs, such as websites, newsletters, writing software, graphics programs, advertising, taxes, etc.

In addition, one of the big-name retailers requires exclusivity, and all of them have terms of service and rules and regulations that make it challenging and time-consuming for an indie author to navigate the publishing world.

Most of us would MUCH rather spend our time creating more stories for YOU, rather than trying to jump through the hoops at the retailers. Buying direct from your favorite authors (where available) helps ensure that an author you love is not subject to unexplained account closures, withholding of royalties, censorship, and other issues that can affect their livelihood.

I've experienced ALL of these. By buying direct, you help put control of my work back in my hands - and I can continue to write more.

Either way, thank you for supporting me! I understand buying direct doesn't work for everyone and even if you use the retailers to buy my books, I appreciate you!

Happy reading,

Nyx

https://www.nyxhalliwell.com/books

YOU'RE INVITED!

Do you have a passion for my stories?
Want more from my characters?
How about early access to ALL my new releases?
My reader community is for YOU!

Try my **Cozy Corner community** for a month! It's ONLY $5 - you're buying me a coffee - and in return, you get all these perks:

Writing Updates so you know what's in the works and how soon you can get it

Special Content, including episodes in my various worlds, character interviews, alternate endings/deleted scenes, future story plot ideas, and cover reveals

Early Access to new stories - I always have multiple books in the works and I release a chapter(s) early before the stories are a available at retailers

Coupons for discounts to <u>my online store</u>

Pics of my pets (all are rescues and they "help" me write and edit)!

You're invited! What are you waiting for?

www.nyxhalliwell.com

Don't miss the next exciting adventure! Sign up for Nyx's Cozy Clues Mystery Newsletter.

And check out these magical stories:

Sister Witches of Raven Falls Special Collection

Confessions of a Closet Medium Cozy Mystery Series

Sister Witches of Story Cove Complete Set

MEET NYX

USA TODAY Bestselling Author Nyx Halliwell grew up on TV shows like *Buffy the Vampire Slayer* and *Charmed*, and loves writing stories as much as she loves baking and crafting. She believes in magick and that we each carry it inside us.

Connect with Nyx today to see pictures of her pets and to be the first to know about new stories and sales! www.nyx-halliwell.com

Thank you for reading this story! It is an honor and a privilege to write books for you. I'm an indie author and every fan is important to me. I pour my heart into each story and do my best to bring you a delightful escape from the real world.

I hope you enjoyed this book, and if so, would you mind leaving a review at your favorite retailer? Or share your enjoyment of it with a friend or family member? I'd really appreciate it, and reviews help other readers find books they will love, too.

Readers are the key to my success - not a traditional publishing deal (had four), an agent (had two), or a publicity team (yep, you guessed it, had several of those as well.)

Those of you who read my books and love my characters and worlds, and who then tell others, are like the best of friends. I adore you and will keep writing if you keep reading!

If you'd like to learn about my other books, sales, and

special promotions, please sign up for my newsletter at www.nyxhalliwell.com.

Support me directly (no retailer taking their cut), grab special edition box sets, and get new releases before they are out at retailers by visiting my store https://www.nyxhalli well.com/books. I have sales and offer NEW RELEASES early! Check it out.

Last but not least, if you enjoy grittier, but still fun, urban fantasy, paranormal romance, or romantic suspense, visit my pen name http://www.mistyevansbooks.com to see those books.

Thank you for supporting my dream.

Blessed be,

Nyx 🖤